Sansan

Her foster parents were cold, unloving. It was Sansan who rose before dawn to stand in line for food, who chopped the fuel, cleaned the house, and washed the clothes. Throughout the year there were "volunteer" labor details: smelting scrap metal in a schoolyard furnace, carrying fertilizer for the rice paddies. At school there was the constant problem of political acceptability, so that she learned to speak and act with quick-witted conformity. Sick some of the time, hungry much of the time, her naturally stubborn character toughened. Yet her humor and her essential tenderness were undiminished. All these qualities were needed when the time came for her to leave the only kind of life she had ever known—to risk a hazardous passage to an unknown border to be reunited with her real mother.

Other Avon Books by
Bette Bao Lord

Spring Moon

EIGHTH MOON

The True Story of A Young Girl's Life in Communist China

SANSAN, AS TOLD TO
BETTE BAO LORD

AVON
PUBLISHERS OF BARD, CAMELOT, DISCUS AND FLARE BOOKS

AVON BOOKS
A division of
The Hearst Corporation
959 Eighth Avenue
New York, New York 10019

First Avon Printing, July, 1983

AVON TRADEMARK REG. U. S. PAT. OFF. AND IN
OTHER COUNTRIES, MARCA REGISTRADA, HECHO EN
U. S. A.

Printed in the U. S. A.

WFH   10   9   8   7   6   5   4   3   2   1

To Grandmother

Chapter One

Finally! The train started to move and within a few seconds I was out of their sight. But I could still see them standing underneath the train window: the white-haired old man, so desperately thin that as a child I used to believe Papa's chest was two wooden washboards; and, by his side, Mama, much younger, too short and too plump. As soon as I had boarded, they huddled together and cried openly. Yet no tears would come to my eyes. Out of kindness I rubbed my eyes red but still could not squeeze out a tiny tear of good-bye. I was so ashamed. I owed them that much.

As the train pulled out of the new Peking station, I sat and wondered about myself, my stubborn nature and my pitiless heart. How cold I had learned to be. I had not been close to them for many, many years, but I grew up in their home as their only child, calling them "Mama" and "Papa" without knowing they were not my real mother and father until just last year. I should have been gentle at parting. They looked so hurt and helpless; they had even forgotten to be angry. Since my decision to go to Hong Kong and my mother, they had often accused me of being ungrateful and mean, but not until the station did I feel a flicker of guilt.

Alone with the strangers on the crowded train, my thoughts skimmed the past and the future.

I hoped that Mother was not seriously ill and that the operation was truly a success. I thought of her beautiful face that I had memorized from the pictures; how I wished that I could have taken those pictures with me. Some of them Mother herself had probably forgotten. My favorite was one taken in the park during the first year of her marriage; it must have been summertime, for her mandarin dress was light and she held an umbrella over her left shoulder to shade her from the sun. Her skin would be very white.

It probably seemed very strange to all of them that I should love someone I had never really known. Yet I could not have been more positive or certain of any action than when I decided to leave the only people and the one place I had known in my lifetime for a future with someone who left me when I was only a year-old baby. They thought they would sway me with political doctrines. How foolish they were. What did I care for governments? I would have journeyed anywhere to be with my real family; had Mother lived in China, India, Spain or the North Pole, it would have made no difference.

The Chinese say that it takes one hundred keys to open one hundred locks, but the key for me was simply the desire to reunited with my true family. I didn't blame the others for not understanding—my feelings had no logical explanation but were deeply rooted in my heart.

They hated me for leaving China to go to America. They couldn't understand that I wasn't forsaking China for America. I was only going to my mother.

I worried about how I would look for our first meeting, and searched for my likeness in the window: at seventeen, I was getting bald—too many years of corn-husk muffins and little else. I tried hard to comb my hair to hide the glossy forehead. What good were my long, long black braids when they hung from the center of my head? I was glad that my cheeks were pink and my skin was clear; ironically, I had the long siege of fever to thank for that. I didn't resemble my family of the pictures. All their faces were shaped like almonds; mine was still childishly round. I hoped the old proverb was true, that if people live together long enough they grow in each other's likeness, for I wanted to look like my new-found elder sisters.

As the train sped along the tracks, I wondered about America, where my family was living. I had studied its history in school many times, but I recalled little: America was separated from England a long time ago; a giant avenue was called Wall Street because the settlers had once erected a wall to keep out the Indians, and now the street housed American capitalists; the great Negro singer Mr. Robeson defected to Russia because of racial prejudice against the black man; the once world-famous child actress Shirley Temple was now a destitute waitress after losing her money on the stock market. I also remembered a comedy skit I once saw in the theater about a party at the White House. All the Western leaders were there playing with hula hoops, and the American President Eisenhower wore a "peace" coat that was cut in the shape of a bomb. The festivities went on throughout the night while masses of the unemployed workers watched on television.

Aside from these random things, I knew little about America except for political theories. However, on the development of capitalism and Communism I could easily talk for seven days and seven nights. But I did not always believe what I learned in politics class. I could only guess that America was either very rich or very poor—otherwise the party would not dwell upon it so much.

My thoughts were interrupted by a pock-marked young man across the aisle.

"Excuse me, Comrade. Can you please tell me if lunch will be served today?"

"I'm sorry, I don't know. While I was at the station I asked the man in the information booth and he could not tell me either. I suggest you ask the conductor when he passes through again."

"Thank you, Comrade."

I felt sorry for the man. A severe case of smallpox had made him extremely ugly.

He learned later that we were not eligible to eat lunch that first day in the dining car because we had just gotten on the train. New passengers are never served the first meal but must wait until the next one. I wasn't very hungry anyway. The other passengers could buy up to two pieces of bread at six cents* each and a cup of tea for five cents that afternoon. The purchases did not require the usual ration coupons, but every item was approximately double the normal price.

The pockmarked man was quite friendly, but I did not wish to talk, wanting only to think and survey the passing countryside. Nevertheless, I did not wish to appear rude, and chatted with him awhile before excusing myself for a short nap. I learned that he was going to see his wife in Canton. When he asked about my destination, I thought it best not to tell him that I was leaving China and going to Hong Kong; so I said that I too was going to visit a relative in Canton. When I was alone again, I slouched down in my reserved seat and looked pensively out the window. As we went further south the scenery was more and more lovely. The mountains were not tall, but a graceful rolling green. In the distance I could see farmers working the fields as the sun slipped beneath the horizon.

From the window these fields were an orderly and peaceful painting. But my own experiences brought back the bitterness of the back-breaking work and the nightmare of the hole. More than anything else in this world I hated the hole, a pit

*There are 100 cents in a yuan, 2.25 yuan to one U.S. dollar. B. L.

of decaying human waste, covered by a swarming blanket of dirty black flies, vomiting waves of pungent stench. I wondered how many times I had been forced to visit the hole that first summer on the farm, to squat by the brink, a newspaper clutched in my hand, fanning away the flies that would light on my face, hair, arms, everywhere.

The images of the farms reminded me that while I was journeying to Hong Kong, my dearest friends were on their way to labor service on still another farm. How I would miss them. I touched my cloth bag beside me on the seat and fingered the tin box that Skinny Monkey had given me several nights before. I would never treasure any gift more than the chicken her family had sacrificed for my farewell dinner.

I wondered about Chocolate. Who was going to pry her from her studies now? I smiled when I recalled my greatest feat—persuading her to see *The Three Musketeers* four times with me.

Without her and big Mah I probably would not have lived through my first attack of dysentery at the farm.

As for Big Nose, I didn't want to think about him.

A familiar song from the loudspeaker on the train interrupted my thoughts to bring back memories of the happy times I had had at the song fests in school. I would surely miss the ''no end'' sessions when we took turns trying to sing songs without having to repeat any that others had sung before. I was often the winner, and must have known a thousand songs.

I would teach songs to my sisters and in return I hoped they would help me to learn English. I would work very hard to learn the new language and to study for school. I would be a dutiful and good daughter.

To my adoptive parents I had been a dutiful daughter only, always careful to do my household chores, but never an easy person to live with. Too proud and too intolerant. I could be worse at times than an old spinster fixed in her habits. But now there was a new beginning for me, and I would try to be less stubborn.

As I lay in my berth at night awaiting sleep, I looked at the cloudless sky and the eighth moon seemed to be traveling with me. It was a very special night, August 15, when each year, according to the Chinese lunar calendar, the moon is at its fullest and families traditionally come together to celebrate the annual holiday. At last, in 1962, after sixteen years, I was on my way to be with my own family. I smiled at the eighth moon and was asleep.

The train trip from Peking to Canton took two days, and as we neared our destination I could see that conditions were increasingly better. The peddlers in the southern stations were selling foods that I hadn't seen in Tientsin for at least a year. The sellers did not ask for ration coupons; they were selling on the black market, knowing the officials were lax. I usually bought a hard-boiled egg at the stops, and a few of them were bad and smelled. Nevertheless, I was eating better than I had in Tientsin. Milk was available on the train if I ordered one day in advance. It came in a soup with bean curds. We were served rice and noodles, and as we neared Canton we ate high-quality rice such as I remembered from when I was much younger. There was only a little vegetable in each portion, but I was happy to have the delicious white rice. I could have eaten several more orders at mealtime, but each passenger was allowed only one portion.

At the last stop before Canton, an old woman with bound feet boarded the train and walked past me with small, unsteady steps, pulling herself along the backs of the seats. It could have been Grandmother. I didn't want to think of her alone in her basement, pulling herself up the stairs with the rope.

Without her there would have been no story to tell.

Chapter Two

The first memory I have is of Papa cradling me in his arms and soothing my sore eyes with his gentle and moist tongue. I was very sick and we were journeying from Shanghai in Tientsin on a boat without a doctor or medicine. Although we were leaving our ancestors' home, we were not unhappy about moving north, because Papa had a new position as an accountant in a shoe factory owned by a classmate of one of our closer relatives. The jobs in postwar Shanghai had been uncertain as was our future.

His qualifications were respectable enough, but hardly in keeping with the promise of his family name. He was the forgotten son of a former secretary of the navy. Now, at fifty, he was taking us north for a new start, leaving behind only a succession of petty business enterprises. A few years earlier he had suddenly married, late in life. He wanted someone with whom he could live out his later years.

Like Papa, Mama was also an unnoticed member of a distinguished family. Her parents were divorced while she was still an infant, and she was raised by a second mother, and then by an even younger third mother. Grandfather was married three times and life was confusing, full of female intrigues and pampered half-brothers and half-sisters in the old-fashioned household. Mama didn't have anyone to turn to, least of all her father. He was a spoiled and brilliant mandarin who cared little about daily affairs, much less the problems of a plain and average number-two daughter of his first wife. Mama thus knew few kindnesses at home and felt no individuality as a young woman. By thirty, she was well prepared to enter into an arranged marriage.

It was considered a good and successful proposition—both of good families with only small claims on life.

The move to Tientsin in 1948, when I was three, was therefore a happy one for all, our only complaint being the harsh northern climate. Our new home was the first floor of a house occupied by a family named Kwan, and I had a room with many large windows. I loved to sit and look out into the garden, where the Kwans' amah worked on the fruit trees, or peer down the road to where Papa would return from work. His thinning gray hair and gaunt build made him look like a grandfather, and his slow walk, with back bent and head down, was easy to recognize. My amah would clean my face, straighten my dress and carry me to my parents' room just in time for me to greet him and receive my present. In those days, Papa never failed to bring me fruit or candy or something I liked every night.

When I was older I was allowed to go out and play by myself. I usually went upstairs to visit with Little Kwan and his many toys. Although I was often invited to stay for dinner, my parents never were; sometimes I even wondered if the Kwans knew whose little girl I was. But then, I was much more popular with everyone than my parents were, and they didn't visit much at all.

All our neighbors loved me, and many called me Little Garlic Face because I was considered very cute and had only a snub of garlic for a nose. I used to wear a yellow bathing suit on sunny days and strut up and down our neighborhood waiting for people to invite me in for a chat or a sweet. If a stranger saw me in my swimsuit, he would always stop and comment on how lovable I was, and I would reply cleverly to prove that I was also very intelligent. How unhappy I was when I outgrew my summer trademark.

Those happy days blended into one another without much to remember: I played, waited for Papa, ate dinner and fell asleep. Life seemed to go on like this forever, until the soldiers came. One morning when I was four, I got up and was going upstairs to trade a pet butterfly for a silkworm when Mama stopped me: "Don't go upstairs anymore!"

"Why?" I asked.

"The Kwans have soldiers in their apartment," she replied, "and I just don't want you to go up there. Now go back and play in your own room."

I didn't understand at all and was very jealous of Little Kwan's new playmates. I could hear their footsteps on my ceiling and their muffled voices and longed to sneak upstairs to join them. But I dared not disobey, and I remained in our apartment for several days until finally the footsteps and voices were gone and I was allowed out again.

The next morning we were awakened by loud poundings and desperate cries of "Let me in!" Papa was first at the door and recognized the Kwan Amah's voice. "It's me—Amah. Hurry! Open the door." He quickly undid the latch and Amah almost fell in. White and trembling, she explained that the civil war had reached the city and the fighting might reach our street at any moment. Mama ran and locked herself in the bathroom, where she stayed for hours, emerging only when we no longer heard any noise from the streets.

For several days, Papa did not go to work but stayed at home. Both Mama and Papa were frightened and went about the house whispering worries I did not quite hear. Unlike them, I was not at all afraid. I thought the sounds of war outside were just like a movie or a game. Although Mama often cried in fear, I never did. I was the star of this war adventure and a star would never cry. I was the brave soldier at night when we had to sleep underneath our beds on the hard floor for fear of stray bullets coming through the window.

One night we were aroused by a constant tapping on the window. Cautiously Papa went over to investigate. It was a lone and dirty soldier with big eyes, begging for an old pair of pants and a shirt so that he could take off his Nationalist uniform. He pleaded for his life, but Papa told him to leave before he got us into trouble. The soldier tapped a little more and then must have crawled away.

The fighting ended soon after that incident. From my window I saw factory workers marching, beating drums and shouting as if they were celebrating a holiday. I wasn't allowed out for a few days, and when I was finally permitted to leave the apartment, I rushed upstairs to exchange stories with Little Kwan, but found the household busily packing. Mr. Kwan explained that they had to leave to follow the Nationalist soldiers and would probably be back someday soon. When I asked why, he said that the Communist soldiers had taken over his factory and he no longer had a job.

Now I no longer had an upstairs playing companion and was lonely, but soon my parents decided to send me off to nursery school, where I could play with other children. School was wonderful, with many friends and snacks of milk and cookies every day. My face was plump and full of dimples, my body neither fat nor skinny, but quite tall for four years and particularly suited for the stage. I was often chosen to represent our school in city competitions, and after one performance, my name was even mentioned in the newspapers. I then began to dream of being a famous and beautiful dancer. I practiced every day, kicking my legs until they touched my forehead, and turning circles on one foot, and taking graceful bows.

I grew very proud, and even haughty, when I was accepted in the best elementary school in Tientsin at the early age of five. I wore my Nan Chung school badge every day and bragged often of my activities in school. I carefully avoided the subject of grades, because I did not study and was embarrassed about my low marks. Nevertheless, I was still chosen to welcome all important and foreign visitors to our model school with a speech and a bouquet of flowers. I met Ho Chi Minh, Chen Yi, and many foreigners from Africa and Latin America. Once my picture appeared in a Russian magazine.

During those years I enjoyed every minute of school, except for composition class and occasional fights with my classmates. My sharp tongue and stubborn manner got me into fights, but I forgot them as quickly as I started them. One time I did linger over a squabble. I don't remember the original issue, but a girl from my block insisted on renewing an argument after school, and I refused. She tagged after me and called me names, but I said nothing. Finally she shouted, ''Where's your mother? Where's your *real* mother?''

"What do you mean?" I asked. "My mother's at home. You know that."

"That's what you think," she scoffed. "Your real mother hated you and left you. She didn't want you—"

"That's a lie! You stop telling lies," I shouted.

"If I am telling a lie, then why, Chin-yee, do your friends call you Sansan [Three-three]? If you are number three, then where are children number one and two? Explain that!" She sneered and ran away.

I thought about her words and walked slowly all the way home. I worried about her accusations for many days and finally had the courage to ask Mama about them. She assured me that I was her child, and that my nickname was Three-three because I was born in the third month on the sixth day, which is three and three. I didn't think about this problem again for a long time.

I was a child who didn't know the difference between the sky and the earth. I only knew about being popular in school and making up dreams. My dreams were usually about dancing and the theater, but in others I was someone else, a person about whom I had read or heard a lovely story. One of my favorite tales was of a white-haired girl, a beautiful farmer's daughter who was persecuted by her landlord and made to endure many indignities. At first the landlord loved the girl and wanted her to be his concubine; but she spurned him, and now his revenge made her life unbearable. Finally she ran to the mountains and lived the life of a hermit, with the trees and the animals as her only companions. She was resourceful and made a very comfortable home and enjoyed the peace of the streams and the skies. After a while her hair turned from ebony black to white because she could not make salt to eat in the mountains. In 1949 she watched Mao's soldiers drive the landlords away and the people rejoicing. She came down from her retreat and returned to her father's home. Her beauty had not been marred; her white hair made her even more striking. Soon she met a handsome young man, and they fell in love and married.

I loved this story and others of unhappy people whose lives were changed completely by fate. In many of the stories I read, "fate" was the Communist revolution, but the new government affected my life very little during my elementary-school years. Around our neighborhood I heard praise for Mao because he had replaced the English street names with Chinese names, and at school I learned about the new regime's campaigns. But these policies were merely lessons to be studied and only occasionally would they concern young students personally: I remember contributing old shoes for the soldiers in Korea, and Papa being detained for a week of questioning during the Five-Anti Campaign, which was launched during 1952 primarily to wipe out abuses in business through investigations of tax evasion, cheating on government contracts, stealing state property, stealing state secrets and bribery.

One of my teachers was also questioned during this campaign. I found Teacher Wu camped on a chair in the middle of the school corridor one morning; he was sitting there like a statue. I approached to ask what he was doing when an older student grabbed me by the arm and shuffled me along, whispering, "His father was a counterrevolutionary and owned a gun. Therefore he must sit in public and contemplate his own political thinking to see whether he has been corrupted by his bad father. Don't go near him."

For three days Teacher Wu sat there while students stared and gossiped. On the fourth day the chair and the man were missing, and I never heard of him again.

Although I was puzzled by such events, I thought the new policies were good. First, they had enabled us to buy furniture we needed for our new apartment at bargain prices, as many wealthy people were selling their possessions during the Five-Anti Campaign to avoid suspicion. Secondly, the government took over the schools and made them free, so my parents could no longer reprimand me for my poor grades by complaining of the money they spent for the expensive Nan Chung.

Despite these advantages and the fact that under the new government controls our new apartment cost only six yuan per month, our family finances did not seem to improve. Mama began night courses in accounting so that she too might get a job. Papa began to nag more and more about money; he had been earning about two hundred yuan per month but now got only sixty. I no longer got presents each night. And we all had to be more careful about our ration coupons. Previously we had surplus coupons at the end of the month, which we often sent to friends. But now coupons were budgeted as closely as money and we hoarded goods that we feared would soon be rationed. I remember that Papa bought over two hundred fifty bars of soap for us to keep. Nevertheless, we continued to live comfortably, if a little more carefully.

The first major impact on my life occurred when Mama got a job keeping the books for an export-import company and there was no one to walk me to school and back. Our new home was quite far away from Nan Chung, and I was only eight, too young to travel the distance alone. Therefore, Mama and Papa decided to board me in the home of a distant relative, Aunt Number Nine, who lived close to the school. Weekdays I lived with her and her large family and returned to my home only on weekends and holidays.

At first I was upset, for I didn't want to leave home. I thought it was wrong to live away from one's parents, but I knew there was no other way to solve the problem. I missed my parents and my own room, but soon learned to enjoy being in a home with sisters and brothers.

Aunt Number Nine was extremely skinny and short, but she was so kind to everyone that I used to think her tiny frame could never hold such a large heart. She was a timid person and devoted to her husband, three daughters, one son, and especially to her invalid mother-in-law. It was characteristic of her to accept me like another daughter. Few people would take an extra child into an already overcrowded family.

The house was only one story high and enclosed by a high wall covered with ivy. It was a very beautiful home. I shared a bedroom with the three daughters, but the bed was big and comfortable. Although I lived with them, I didn't play much with the children because none of them were my age, some much older and some much younger.

Most of my playmates were still from my class. One morning I got to school a little early and stayed outside to play with some friends. When it was time to go inside we gathered together, and on our way in we spotted a boy nicknamed Crybaby sniveling on the steps. He was holding on to a scraped knee and pouring tears. I was tired of his lack of control; he was always crying over every little fall or accident. That day I decided I was going to do something about it, and ran in front of the group. I sat down beside him and started to braid his hair. My audience loved it and all laughed and pointed at the victim, who sat passively and hid his face in the crook of his arm. I had almost completed the eighth little pigtail when the janitor came out of the building and peered angrily at us. We couldn't stop giggling, and some, convulsed, had to sit down on the ground. I thought that the man would soon appreciate our playfulness, and I waited for a change of expression. But his face remained the same. His eyes took all of us in, and then he shouted, "How can you children be playing silly pranks when Stalin has died?"

I was stunned and ashamed and tears came to my eyes. Everyone else was crying too. We had never met this Russian leader, but we knew that he was a good man, a great man who had helped his people. And now he was dead.

All students knew of Russia and Stalin because Communism and international politics were taught in school. There was also a party-sponsored organization called Young Pioneers. At first membership was confined to excellent students, and thus was far beyond my expectations; but within a couple of years practically all students wore red cotton scarves, the symbol of the Young Pioneers. However, I still was not one of them; a nervous teacher continually blackballed me because I fidgeted in class. I began to worry, not because I was missing private meetings or even special trips, but because I was concerned about my future. I noticed that students who were not members by graduation were not assigned to good junior high schools. When, at the age of ten, I finally received my red scarf at the end of my fifth year of school, I was very relieved.

The secret weekly meetings of the organization were, as I suspected, rather boring: usually a teacher would speak on some disciplinary problem at school, then the students would sing a few songs or learn a patriotic slogan or two. My friends and I sat together to chat and to caution each other if a teacher was approaching. Occasionally we would hear stories about student virtues or of life in other countries. I remember one story about a black boy named Joe, who lived in Chicago, America. He was a very good boy and often helped his uncle pick potatoes. One day, the uncle was so pleased with his nephew's work that he gave him a nickel. Joe was very, very happy, and went to town to buy his favorite bubble gum. That night, the "Three K's" (Ku Klux Klan) came and accused the child of whistling at a white girl. Before the boy could deny the charge, the masked men in white sheets wired him to a rock and dropped him in the Tai-lu River. Joe's blood colored the river red. At the end of the story, we all learned a stanza of the poem "Why Is the Tai-lu River Red?"

> Mother asked God why?
> (Gesture to the right)
> God did not answer.
> Mother asked the heavens why?
> (Gesture to the left)
> The heavens did not speak.

Within the Young Pioneers there were several offices. There was a captain and four vice captains below him, each in charge of a committee. The committees generally considered the selection of new members, literature and physical education, political training and sanitation. The officers were elected by the members, but I abstained the only time I participated in an election. We were to choose a captain for political training, and our teacher nominated a boy whose political thinking was sound but who had a face full of pimples and a sour disposition. No one liked him. After the teacher counted our secret ballots and discovered that his candidate had not received enough votes, he said, "Those who oppose Yen, please raise your hands." No one wanted to be an open dissenter, and all kept still.

"Since no hands were raised, Yen is obviously elected."

I was disappointed that Pimple Face got elected but soon became less and less concerned over student politics, for I had other problems to brood over. I had changed from a cute and healthy child to a short and rather plump girl, and no longer had leading roles but stood on stage with the chorus. Eventually even my pride had to admit that my hopes of stardom would never come true. All my dreams burst.

I was also worried about Mama, whose moods became more unpredictable and more extreme. Once when I was about nine, I came home after studying at a friend's house and she used a bamboo stick to hit me for being late. When Papa tried to intervene, she merely hit him too. She finally stopped only when the stick broke. Another time she offered to take me to the movies, an unexpected treat. Afterward, she asked me not to tell where we had been, but I was young and forgot and bubbled about the good show as soon as I reached home. My small hands bore the marks of her hairbrush for days.

Yet I knew she must love me very much because she was always possessive and would never consent to the many requests from her friends and my teachers that I become their goddaughter. I just didn't understand Mama's moods. I thought that her bad temper was a result of her glandular disorder and tried to be sympathetic. Her whole body would swell up until it looked like a gigantic *man to* (a doughy Chinese bread). As much as I wanted to be understanding about her illness, I avoided being with her, for she took little care to make herself presentable when she was so afflicted. She never bothered to iron her dresses or comb her hair; I hated to walk with her—her unclosed collar, her shapeless body, her immense and untidy appearance made me ashamed that she was my mother.

Papa also was afraid of her unpredictable tempers. He constantly feared that she would leave him; he couldn't stand the thought of having to fend for himself.

As my sixth year of school drew to a close, I tried to forget about my own troubles and concentrated on getting good final grades so that I would be assigned to junior high school. For the first time I studied very hard. After the exams were over, I was able to go to Peking to visit relatives and have a vacation. I loved the capital and especially the famous university. It was then that I started dreaming about going there for my college education. While I was in Peking, I received the news that I had been assigned to the Chi Lee School. It was not my first choice, but it was a good school because until recently it had been limited to the children of party members. I returned to Tientsin with visions of a new beginning at the Chi Lee School.

Despite these worries, I thought life was simple and daily living uncomplicated. I believed that if a person was alive, anything was possible. Actually, daily life at that time was nothing but drying dishes and washing chopsticks. I often thought home was not ideal and sometimes wanted to run away. Many times I dreamed of carrying an umbrella and climbing mountains. That would be wonderful. I was so small and very innocent.

Chapter Three

The Chi Lee School was a cluster of buildings with traditional Oriental red-tile roofs and did look rather impressive from afar. Sitting inside, I was not at all certain that the old walls would not at any moment yawn and fall asleep on top of us all. Outside of an occasional feeling of uneasiness while wall-gazing, I was proud and content and satisfied to be there. I felt guilty that my only passport to the school was luck and vowed with determination to forget my earlier ways and to work hard for good grades. Every time I thought about my new life I felt very adult and wise. This analysis of myself was certainly a sign that I would accomplish great things and gave me an extremely regulated outlook on my life. The dream of theatrical success was gone, but my vision of an active life in school and eventual renown in some yet unknown field was quickly taking its place.

During the first few months of classes, the school launched a campaign to reduce illiteracy that gave me an excellent opportunity to test my resolutions. I worked hard to learn more new words and even found myself helping others.

That's how I became friends with Mah. Although she was fifteen, four years older than I, she like other peasant children, had started school late and needed some extra help with her homework.

I guess we became friends because she was older and looked after me as if I were a younger sister or even, sometimes, her child. We certainly didn't have much in common: she was an athlete and was a star racer in school; I hated gym classes. She was never quite clean and I was very fastidious. She was not ambitious and I had many dreams. But we both liked to laugh and play practical jokes. I shall never forget the time she sprinkled salt on a live porcupine and sealed him in a box which was carefully hidden under the bed of a newly married cousin. Every time we thought about how the young couple must have been baffled by the coughing of an "old woman" in their room, we could not stop laughing.

School for us was work but also a time to get together. At first we had many hours to ourselves, but one day the political teacher called the class for a meeting. He announced that there might be a program to combine education and labor service in schools and asked for discussion and ideas from students about such a campaign. Some older students began the meeting and gave their approval. I thought it would be horrible and raised my hand. "I don't think such a program would be good. After all, we are students and our first duty is to study. If we are to work at labor details, our study time will be cut down and we cannot continue to do as well in school. I don't like the idea of such a combination. I think students ought to study and leave the labor work until we have finished our schooling."

There was a silence. I sensed that I had not said exactly the right thing, even for someone like me. However, four others got up and supported my views. Then the teacher regained the floor and said, "It is obvious that all of you realize the importance of such a movement. Only a handful are not enthusiastic. Perhaps these students do not realize the full implications of such a proposal and only see the short-range effect of such a change."

He was looking straight at me and I had the odd feeling that I must have looked very unusual. I looked down to make sure that my simple white blouse and blue skirt had not been mysteriously replaced by high-heeled shoes and mandarin dress with exaggerated slits, of the type worn only be actresses and extraodinary people who do not mind being condemned.

Finally his eyes left me and took in the entire group.

"Let me tell you about the philosophy behind such a combination movement. When you have heard the sound reasons and motives for this change, you will no longer doubt. So far, you as students have learned only through books and other people's writings. It is now time for you to turn to actual experience. You may have read that the sea is blue, but if you have not seen the sea, how can you be sure? You can only be sure of something after you yourself have experienced it.

"Now is the time for you to touch and feel what you have up to now only read about. It is time for you to broaden your experience and outlooks.

"First, you will learn about the life and the thinking of other groups of citizens. This you will learn by actually doing the work they do, and when you have toiled at their jobs you will understand their worries and language. In capitalist countries, the people would not be concerned about these things because their societies are made up of different classes, each understanding only his worries and his language. Therefore these people will be in constant conflict. The Chinese must learn about all their peoples—they must learn to understand the worker, the farmer, the teacher, and so on.

"Second, you will learn to protect your country. Through labor you will develop your muscles and your bodies. Then if China is ever in a war, you can rise to help. You must be strong enough to raise the gun and fight the enemy.

"Lastly, members of a socialist country should be all-round citizens. We cannot all be intellectuals and know only of books. China must have intellectuals, yes—but these intellectuals must also be workers. Everyone should be able to lift the pen as well as the gun."

His speech made sense and I felt a bit ashamed of my remarks because I knew that while upholding education, I was also trying to conserve my own free time and vacations. I had been selfish and did not want to see school projects deprive me of my own time.

When we were dismissed, the class was anxious to get started on this new movement. We were all prepared to become all-round citizens of China.

Our first chance was to produce steel at furnaces built in the schoolyard. The project was started with the help of two steelworkers who came to supervise the boys in building four furnaces. The boys first dug large holes about three feet deep, and then constructed a square brick box on top. When completed, the furnaces looked like squat rectangular miniature houses with no windows and a small door. After these were in place, the entire school was assigned to collect metal to feed these four brick houses. We brought pots and pans from home, scoured garbage dumps for metal scraps, and cut down metal fences about town and replaced them with wooden pickets. After the raw material was gathered, the girls were assigned to breaking up our hoard into small bits with rocks and passing them from hand to hand along the long queue of students to the boys who shoveled the bits and fed them to the fiery hot-coal stomachs of the furnaces. The first day at the job made me feel happy; I had an excuse to stay longer at school with friends and I was actively helping my country. As we pounded the metal, we talked and sang patriotic songs. It was great fun for about an hour. Then my arm hurt—so did my back, my legs, my feet; my spirits were laid out on the ground, where I longed to be. The atmosphere changed from that of a class outing to "let's finish and go home for dinner and rest."

We finally finished that day, but the monotony of drumming small bits for the schoolyard furnaces continued for many months. We were not allowed to move away from our station in the chain of working students, we had no energy to sing, and we did not talk for fear of being called loafers.

At the start of the project we worked after school hours, which were from eight to four, but after the furnaces were built, students were assigned to daily eight-hour shifts that manned the furnaces twenty-four hours a day, seven days a week, including holidays and vacations. I had turns at all three shifts—from six in the morning to two in the afternoon, from two to ten at night, and from ten to six in the morning. Sometimes I was not even dismissed after my shift, but was asked to work overtime. We continued to attend classes before or after these working hours.

At the end of the project the school paid us each four yuan for our toil. Papa added another fifteen cents and I bought a new pen. This pen, and whatever equivalent each schoolmate got, were all we had to show for the work we devoted to the four schoolyard furnaces. The steel we made was practically useless and had to be sent for reprocessing at the regular steel factories, and the families who had contributed their kitchenware now haunted stores for replacements.

Throughout the entire period we worked at the steel factories, I was very indignant and believed that it was my duty to inform the Education Bureau that the Combination of Labor and Education Movement was not producing results. I had no new insights into the life of a steelworker; I was merely exhausted and unhappy. Every night, after the habitual long day at school desk and school furnace, in the few minutes before I fell asleep I thought about the letter I would write to the Bureau. The letter would stop all this nonsense. If the Education Bureau knew the real situation, I was positive the movement would be ended. I visualized every word.

DEAR COMRADES:

The purpose of a student is to study, and the purpose of vacation is to rest. The rest is to help us prepare for further work in the school year. Why then are students told to work during the vacation?

I do not object to working, but I object to working all the time, especially on my vacation. We have worked six days a week so far.

Sincerely yours,
CHIN-YEE

I wanted to write this letter so badly I could almost form the characters in my sleep. But I was too tired to do anything but fall into bed as soon as I reached home.

During the seventh grade, our class had many such labor-service, or *lao dung*, assignments, but they all were in the city. It was not until summer vacation that we received our first task in the countryside. Although practically everyone had grown rather disillusioned with *lao dung*, all were enthusiastic about going to the farm. The political teacher told us to return home and pack for a ten-day assignment in the country. We were given free bus tickets and were all to meet the next day at the school to board the bus which would take us there.

Although it meant work during our forty-day summer vacation, the entire class seemed to welcome the change from the same daily routines to a free visit to the countryside. That night I babbled about the trip to Mama and Papa and excused myself early to pack and to think about the coming days. As I lay on my bed and looked out at the sky through my window, I became enchanted by the prospect of being somewhere else, somewhere I had never been. I always thought birds were such lucky creatures because they were free to go anywhere—they merely had to flap their wings and go. Birds didn't have to be rich or get permission; they could fly above the earth and see many different scenes of life below. They could stop and visit so many towns in their lifetime. That night I dreamed I was a bird, flying free and following a breeze to see the placid mountains and serene green plains of the farmlands.

I woke up early the next morning, and packed a change of underwear, an extra pair of cotton pants, a blouse, blanket, washcloth, toothpaste and toothbrush in a carpetbag. I started for school without waking my parents. It was a fine summer day and the sun was, like me, about to start on a journey. I walked, then skipped, and often turned around to walk backward—just to see what I was leaving behind. There were only a few people out, and I owned the entire city.

As soon as I reached school, I looked for Mah. She had a much longer walk than I did, and had probably had to feed her many sisters and brothers before leaving. While I sat around waiting, a grammar-school girl came up to speak to me. She opened her eyes wide to look at me and sighed. "You must have been born under the right stars, for you are old enough to go to the countryside. I'm not in seventh grade yet and have to remain behind. I wish they would let me go—I've never been anywhere except my house and school."

I knew exactly how she felt and sympathized with her, but I could not help saying, "Can you imagine—the school is even paying our fare."

I heard someone call to me from a distance and saw flying pigtails coming toward me. Sure enough, it was Mah. She had even dressed up for the trip. I knew it immediately because she had on her bright-red blouse and bright-green pants; every time she dressed up, she looked worse than if she did not. She was not a pretty girl—her face was too long and her mouth too large—but everyone liked her golden heart. For that reason, no one wanted to be the one to tell her that she had no style sense whatsoever. We once went together to buy a handkerchief. There were many very nice white ones with rolled edges, but she chose one with large red roses and large green leaves.

As she approached, I could tell that she had even taken extra care to braid her long hair properly. She was excited, as I was, and we grabbed each other's waist and bounced off to the bus. The trip took two hours and every minute of it was filled with songs and pranks and laughter. Our teacher sat in front and joined us when we sang. I looked out the bus window to find things that I might never have seen before. Suddenly I saw a little shop with a sign reminding customers to buy their small moon cakes in time for the holidays. How I loved their flaky golden crust and sweet dark filling. I quickly tugged at Mah and pressed her nose in the direction of the disappearing sign. "I can't wait to have moon cakes again. Too bad the full-moon celebration comes only once a year."

"Uh-uh. This year I'm going to hide somewhere and eat my cake. Last time, one of my little sisters came begging and I had to give her a piece," Mah replied.

"At least you have a large family to watch the moon with. I would gladly give a piece of my cake away if I had sisters and brothers. The midautumn festival should be much more fun when there's a lot of family around and not just three people.''

''I guess so,'' Mah mumbled.

''We'll be gone for ten days and come back in time for all the fun. Oh, I'm so happy. I can't wait for the full moon.''

''Me neither,'' said Mah.

The bus soon stopped in front of an abandoned temple and I thought we were to get out and stretch our legs. Instead, our teacher told us to gather our things and form two groups—the boys on the right and the girls on the left. We were then led to different sections of the empty temple.

The girls' side was a huge, dark room that was practically bare except for some worn straw mats and a collection of assorted Buddhas, large and small, but each with a broken arm, head or stomach, sleeping in the carved niches of the walls. The floor was earthen and quite dirty. We claimed our spots, cleaned up the soil around us as best we could, and left our belongings to receive instructions outside. Mah didn't even have time to change from her best outfit. A farmer was waiting to give us our orders.

''Your job for today is to bucket, ferry and dump human fertilizer. You will take it from the reservoir to the fields,'' the farmer told us.

I glanced around without turning my head and saw that my classmates were not surprised by the farmer's words. Actually, why should it surprise us? We knew what happened on farms, that the use of human fertilizer was traditional.

The farmer demonstrated how to handle the buckets and balance one at each end of a bamboo pole. After the farmer's brief talk, and before we started out to work, our teacher stood up and spoke. She reminded us of the philosophy of the Combination of Labor and Education Movement and dwelt on the privilege of participating in China's agricultural program. Then she announced that she would put a red flag at the end of the field and whoever could capture the flag by fertilizing his area first would be the "Hero for Today." Each day there would be a new hero. We all clapped and shouted. What fun—a new game!

Then we started out. My nose and stomach told me how close we were getting to our destination. I looked for Mah's eyes, but when I caught her attention I couldn't smile or even change my expression—my tongue was clenched to the roof of my mouth to block the passage from my stomach. My first impulse was to hold my nose, but I saw no one doing so. Besides, our teacher was leading a song and striding purposefully forward to the fertilizer supply.

Mah and I stayed together. I volunteered to carry the first load. She filled the buckets by dishing the stuff with a large ladle. I adjusted the bamboo pole on my right shoulder, and feeling certain I had the proper balance, I straightened my knees and rose to my full height. I smiled; the front bucket had been lifted off the ground. Then came a splash and a cry from Mah. The rear bucket had dumped its contents all over my trouser legs and Mah's bright-green pants. We yelled and raced toward the river. I knew no amount of water would bring back her "beautiful" pants, and was ready to throw my arms around Mah's big frame and cry. But she laughed and I stopped and looked and laughed also.

We marched back to try again. This time we were more careful and worked that day without another accident. I had mastered the bamboo pole and even could ignore somewhat the strong, dank cloud that enveloped our working area. But I could not ignore the flies that would light on my face whenever my hands were too busy balancing the buckets to brush them away. How I hated those dirty flies!

It was about a mile from the supply area to the rice paddies, but under the scorching summer sun the walk seemed unending. After my first load I was exhausted and lost all enthusiasm for the game and the title of "Hero for Today." My right shoulder was already swollen red and purple, being unaccustomed to the heavy weight and the constant rubbing of the pole. I wanted to pad the sore spot, but I needed my handkerchief to keep my long braids from accidental dunkings in the fertilizer. We were finally dismissed at about six o'clock. I thought I was paralyzed. Every bone and every muscle ached. My skin was raw from the harsh exposure to the sun and my complexion was yellow.

I tried to wash the stench away in the river, but I never felt clean again during our entire stay. Dinner was rice and some salted vegetables. I thought the food terrible, but knew I had eaten a lot when I saw how many ration coupons I had to give up. That night I wrote a short note home telling my parents I had arrived safely and was enjoying the countryside. I certainly was not going to let them embarrass me with reminders of my earlier enthusiasm.

The days dragged on—either a succession of buckets of brownish-yellow muck or constant stepping and pushing on a spade's sharp edge with the right shoe. It was endless. Finally something happened—it rained! We were excused for the entire day, except for some political meetings, and Mah and I and some boys went off to trap fish. We gathered weeds and stalks by the bank and tied them together by armloads. Then the boys rolled up their pants and laid the bunches end to end against the riverbank. We waited on shore. It was so exciting to see a fish caught in our dam, and then the flourish of hands, feet and bodies that dove for the fish. We had so much fun we almost forgot our unpleasant daily routine. That night we had fish with our rice and salted vegetables, played chess, and fell asleep hoping it would rain again tomorrow.

The next day was hot and sunny, as were the rest. I started thinking about home and about baths and soap and food and everything I hadn't appreciated before. I wrote letters at night to my parents, for I was afraid to complain to my classmates or to my teacher. My letters now were filled with longings for home and accounts of our hard labors. I wrote several letters and only received a reply to the last one, which had asked for sixty cents. How spoiled I was then. The food I ate was nourishing enough—after all, it was white rice—but I was so young and very foolish. I wrote for money to buy cookies at the local store. Papa sent me the money, but his letter was cold and unpleasant. I never thought that he would lecture me on my homesickness. He wrote of my weakness and of my lack of discipline. He accused me of missing home only because of hard work, and said that if I were in Peking on vacation, I would not have written in such a tender tone. I was hurt, but I could not feel self-righteous because what he said was probably true.

I soon forgot about the letter because it was time for us to leave—the ten days were up. We awoke with unusual energy and smiled as if we shared a secret. At breakfast, the talk was of the midautumn festival and of moon cakes and of being with our families again. Our gaiety could not be smothered, not even by the announcement of a meeting. We all filed into the room and sat down on the floor in high spirits. An official from the Education Bureau came in. We immediately quieted down and waited for his words. Then he told us, ''You have done a good job while you were here. You have learned and accomplished a great deal. The Education Bureau is proud of the success of *lao dung* in the countryside and wishes to thank you for your help, students.''

We all grew three inches taller and looked around with congratulations for everyone.

''But . . .''

We all turned back toward the official.

''But the job has not been completed. May I have some volunteers for further days of service?''

Not a sound. We were all trying to remember whether we were in a dream or in the room.

The teacher reacted quickly. ''We won't go home until the job's done.''

Everyone, stuttering at first, but growing stronger: ''We won't go home . . . until the job's done. We won't go home until the job's done. WE WON'T GO HOME UNTIL THE JOB'S DONE.''

It was an infectious chant and the room was filled with our enthusiastic yells. We all shouted as if we were rooting for our basketball team. I even banged on the floor.

Our voices were stopped only by the raised hand of the Education Bureau official. He thanked us and asked the teacher to see him outside for further arrangements.

Our eyes followed the teacher across the room and we could hear her steps on the floor. They walked off together and we remained sitting where we were.

I sat there, thinking of nothing and looking at nothing. The room was frozen. The silence was finally shattered by a small, sharp gasp for breath from a corner. We all turned and saw a grown boy helplessly dropping tears. As if on signal, we all cried with passion, like little children.

That night we all sat together under the eighth moon and felt ever so close to one another. It was August 15, the day of the reunion of family. I gazed upon the bright and mysterious moon and felt very old and weary at twelve.

The next morning, I was sick with a severe case of intestinal dysentery and I could barely move from my bed to walk the distance to the outdoor hole. There are two types of dysentery, and I was unlucky enough to get the white variety, which never frees its victims from feelings of extreme urgency. Often the urgency was a false alarm. During the day, I was excused from field work and stationed myself near the hole. At night I had to ask for help. I don't remember how many times a night I would crawl over the sleeping bodies of my classmates in search of Mah and Feng, another friend. Mah would hold me up and guide my steps to the hole while Feng would walk ahead with a flashlight to prevent any unforeseen accidents. They took me for many walks during those nights and never once uttered an embarrassing remark; not even when the trips were false alarms, not even when I didn't reach the hole in time and they had to wash my pants.

They looked after me like two young mothers. Mah even used some of her precious oil coupons to give me extra nourishment. I feel as if I owe them my life. After a few more days of illness, I received permission to return to Tientsin ahead of the others.

A boy from my class named Big Nose was to take me to the bus because I could not walk that far. I didn't know him very well but always admired his dashing looks. At school the boys all wore more or less the same type of blue cotton shirts and pants, yet somehow he always managed to stand out. The same coarse blue shirt looked glamorous because he wore a turtleneck sweater underneath—I learned many years later that the sweater was full of holes and was practically only a neck. His family name was Tsiang but everyone knew him as Big Nose. His nose was not Chinese; it could have belonged to a native of Europe, especially after he grew a hint of a mustache. Because of it, he always played the part of a foreigner in our school plays.

Big Nose came and carefully helped me onto the seat of his bicycle and he pushed me along all the way to the bus station. After we got going he said, "How are you doing, Ice Pop?"

"Ice Pop? Where did you get that name for me?"

"Mah told me about your talking in your sleep during your fever," Big Nose replied. "You kept asking for an ice pop."

We were friends at once. We talked all the way to the bus station about our love of music and the theater. He told me he was going to be an actor and would try to get into the National

Theater School after he finished at the Chi Lee School. I encouraged him because I felt he was a born actor.

When we reached the station, Big Nose wanted to carry me aboard, but I resisted, asserting that I could manage, because I simply hated boys to touch me. I had to compromise, and he held on to my elbow. We waved good-bye.

I did not recognize the bus or the road, yet I knew they were unchanged from our trip out to the countryside. Perhaps it was I that had not remained the same. I concentrated on keeping my stomach together during the bumpy ride. At last we arrived in Tientsin.

I leaned against the seats and helped myself off and searched about for Mama or Papa to help me home. No one I knew was at the station. I couldn't understand it; they both knew I was sick and would be coming home, yet they were not there. I waited until I was sure no one was coming. And started home alone.

Chapter Four

As I walked home alone from the bus station, I decided that my parents were unable to meet me because they both had to volunteer for extra work on Sunday. I was wrong. Mama and Papa were at home entertaining some of their friends, and all were enjoying pears as I walked through the door. My feelings were hurt, but I knew better than to question my parents in front of the guests. Mama came forward and looked me over. "What happened to you? You have turned black."

She didn't even ask about my illness. "The sun was very bright in the fields and we were burned dark." Everyone noticed the color of my skin and remarked what a shame it was that my fair skin had been ruined. Mama then handed me a pear. Before I even finished my first bite of the delicious fruit, I knew I was going to be very sick. I ran from the room and up the stairs to the toilet. Never was I so glad to find it empty of our ten neighbors, who shared the only facility in the apartment building.

Despite my sudden attack and my disappointment at not being met at the station, I was already feeling much better. I was away from the hole and the flies, so numerous you could grab a handful merely by making a fist, and the scrap paper of unknown origin that we used for toilet paper.

I was happy that night to be in the privacy of my own bed, without the company of my cadre. My room was on a landing halfway between the first floor, where Mama and Papa slept, and the second floor. It was a small room with one bed, two chairs, three old trunks and a large wicker basket full of string, rags and other junk. The walls were painted white, the floor was polished cement, and one electric bulb hung low from the ceiling.

Next to my room was the community bathroom, with tub, sink and running water. On the second floor was the community flush toilet and a basin whose running water hadn't worked in anyone's memory. I did our laundry in the tub; the sink was so dirty I never touched it. The small bathroom also served as a storage area: one neighbor piled his coal in one corner and another kept his stove against the wall.

Our house had once been an English-style office building and was considered one of the best apartment houses in our neighborhood.

The next day I went to the hospital. After examining me, the doctor asked angrily why I had waited so long to come in with my serious case. I explained that I was on a labor assignment in the country and had not received permission to come home until yesterday. The doctor gave me a prescription for a very strong medicine and told me to rest.

During the time I spent in bed at home, I thought about the farm and how my friends had cared for me. Mah and Feng had spent their money and their precious coupons for two whole ounces of oil and two eggs, their rations for several weeks. They fried the fish which the boys caught to make me a delicious and nutritious soup of eggs and fish. I cried each time I compared the concern of my friends with the attitude of my own parents.

I supposed they still loved me in their own way. When I was small and cute, they played with me as they would a doll. But once I was grown up, I became just one of the many problems they faced. Now, even without me, getting along with each other and making ends meet seemed too much for them. They didn't have any interest left for me.

My rest lasted for less than a week because school started as usual on September first. I hoped that this new year would be different from the previous one, with labor work during and after school hours and on holidays. I thought the Education Bureau must surely realize that the Combination of Labor and Education Movement was not building better citizens, and I looked forward to a normal student life again.

I couldn't have been more mistaken. Eighth and ninth grades were to be much worse. My hopes for a labor-free school year ended as soon as I learned of my class schedule for the semester. We were going to be more involved in political campaigns than ever; along with my courses in zoology and botany, physics, chemistry, geometry and algebra, physical education, music, Chinese literature and grammar, there was a new class called "political discussion." Beginning in 1957, all students in all schools were assigned to weekly political-discussion groups. At my school, we were allotted to specific groups of approximately fifteen students with one student group leader, and we met for two class periods or more each Wednesday afternoon. The leader would open the meeting by announcing the topic assigned by the political teacher and asking for opinions. A teacher walked around the room with ears open but seldom interrupted the meetings. At first we were all puzzled as to exactly what was expected of us, but soon we all learned and tried to find a way to fulfill our obligations without making a mistake.

It was at a meeting to discuss the violation of classmate Han that I learned a genuine opinion was not appreciated even though you had to speak. At this meeting we were asked our views of Han's violating the rule against social dancing for students. A teacher had discovered music scores for dance tunes in Han's desk, and after scolding him severely, asked that he be reprimanded by his own classmates. I knew Han and knew that he could not dance, but only liked to hum dance tunes. I announced this to my group and argued that Han really did not violate the rule against dancing.

"We as students are not allowed to dance, but it is perfectly proper for adults. So there is nothing really bad about dancing, is there? When Han grows older, he will be allowed to dance. Besides, in this case, Han didn't even dance. He merely hums the tunes, and what can be serious about that?"

I had hardly finished when all hands went up and each person in turn reprimanded me. After that experience, I knew better than to speak my convictions. I realized that while it was not smart to keep quiet and thus arouse suspicion, I was expected to express only opinions that echoed the ones suggested by the group leader. Sometimes it was very hard to find a new way of saying the same thing, and I often spoke up early in the discussion so that no one else could steal my ideas. Later, I discovered an even better method: I would volunteer to take minutes of the meetings, knowing that the recorder was always the last one asked for an opinion. Usually time ran out before the group leader could call on me.

Other students also had opinions which they kept to themselves. On the day on which we were assigned the topic "American Products Are Not Superior to Chinese Goods," the group leader told us that many Chinese inherited the false assumption that American goods were the best from the pre-1949 revolutionary thinking of the bandit Chiang Kai-shek's government. "It is a bad habit; Chinese should not pay homage to foreign goods. Chinese people produce excellent products," etc. Everyone agreed. After the meeting, a student remarked sarcastically under his breath, "American goods are not superior. But there can be no doubt that the Russian goods are the best. Everything American is bad. Everything Russian is wonderful. In the end, we are still looking to foreign things. Russia is a foreign country just like America."

This student was lucky that no one reported him. There was another boy, about fourteen, who had an excellent chance of going on to high school and whose remarks were reported. He had been very discouraged with *lao dung*, and he asked his classmates to explain to him the difference between their work on the farms and the drafted labor gangs of previous emperors. He claimed there was no difference; it meant forced labor whether the government was a dynastic reign or Communist. The philosophy of education and labor couldn't make him believe otherwise.

Nothing happened to him immediately. But a few months later, at graduation, he was assigned to work instead of further education.

In that same year, 1958, another meeting was instituted, called "life discussions." We met with the same fifteen students and the same group leader as the political discussions, but these meetings were not so long or formal. We generally gathered about once every two weeks for twenty minutes, just long enough for everyone to speak up. The purpose of these meetings was to discuss school problems and to air grievances against each other. Often we merely confessed a small offense, such as throwing paper on the floor or speaking in class or forgetting to do homework, so that we could fulfill our obligations without criticizing someone else.

We didn't take these short meetings so seriously as the lengthy political discussions. Yet there were times when the atmosphere was tense. I remember one meeting when a classmate accused another of stealing his pants—a serious offense, for none of us owned more than two or three pairs. The accused boy denied it and began to cry. After the meeting there was much bitterness because nothing was really resolved and suspicions were still lurking around this accused classmate. After two weeks, the pants were returned to the owner's desk, and we never knew who had stolen them.

As a result of both the political and the life discussions, I learned to keep my opinions to myself and seldom spoke out to anyone. Only occasionally would I let slip a minor complaint to one of my best friends. There was nothing really to fear—no one was going to put me in jail or hurt me—but I didn't want to be different from the other students. I didn't want them to criticize me, and I didn't want to appear less cooperative during campaigns and other school activities than my fellow classmates. There were times when I felt compelled to do things against my will. For example, the teacher would often ask for volunteers for extra labor at a factory or at school, and one by one all my classmates would offer their help. I hated the extra work, but I could not be the only one who did not volunteer.

I was disappointed that school activities in campaigns took more and more of my time, but I could not complain because my supervisor at school liked me very much and often gave me a special assignment instead of the usual *lao dung*. While my classmates did heavy labor, I represented our school in making requests from local factories and stores. My job was to borrow equipment for school projects and procure favors from the neighborhood.

As representative I was very successful and generally got what I requested. Small in size and the youngest in my class, I pretended to be innocent and naïve whenever I approached a factory manager. I would ask humbly for favors, never demanding or threatening like other school representatives, who thought that everyone was obligated to contribute to their school projects, and who reported those who did not as backward elements. I would smile and act like a student with a head only for studying and no knowledge of politics or bureaucracy. "I know you will help me; I am very confident now that my request is in your hands." My flattery and innocence were usually successful.

For example, I surprised even my supervisor when I was able to get an early shipment of bowls for our school and gloves for students working at the cement factory. The factories had hundreds of outstanding orders for bowls that they could not fill and the hospital had refused many others who needed gloves for their project.

Besides these special duties, I had to participate in many campaigns, which seemed more and more numerous. Food was getting scarce, and our school decided to raise *mor goo*, a type of Chinese mushroom, for which horse manure is needed as fertilizer. Every morning we students all carried two burlap bags over our shoulders to school—one for books and one for the manure. We would pick up manure on our way to school and dump our haul in the schoolyard before classes.

I had to look happy as I picked up with my bare hands manure freshly deposited by the Tientsin horses. I would be immediately criticized if I made a face or looked with disdain at the fertilizer. After a while I got used to it, for surprisingly, the manure was odorless and it seldom rubbed off on my hands. Not so on rainy days, however.

After weeks of gathering early-morning horse manure, the streets were quite clean and free of these deposits. It became more and more difficult to meet our daily quotas. No matter how I scrambled down the streets to school or trailed after horses, I could no longer fill my book bag. When our group total failed to be a respectable amount, our captain was troubled and angry that his team was not bringing in the most manure. So one day after school, he gathered together his group and announced a manure expedition. We were going to take manure from the local commune.

I was still naïve and asked the captain, "Are you sure the commune will give us their supply?" The captain was annoyed and said that we were going to take it. I was shocked. "Do you mean we are going to steal horse manure from them? What if they catch us?"

The boy looked mean and replied, "Shut up or else I'll wrinkle your face."

Silenced, I followed him and the group to the commune. We crawled under a fence, frantically filled our book bags, and scurried away with our loot. After we deposited the fertilizer at school, the captain came over to me and quite sheepishly asked if I would like a piece of cake.

In addition to picking and stealing horse manure, we had to plant, water and care for the *mor goo* crop. We first tacked up old burlap over the windows to keep out all sunlight from the room assigned for the plants. Then we took turns tending the garden at night. We were all very proud when the harvest finally came up. The *mor goo* were over four inches in diameter, and we looked forward to eating them. Anxiously we harvested the crop, pulling the plants out of the dirt floor and putting them into baskets.

After all the plants were harvested, we eagerly anticipated having *mor goo* for lunch the next day. However, that afternoon our teacher announced that we could buy the school's *mor goo* for five yuan a bag after school. I was furious, but had no choice and paid the five yuan for my bag.

We had so many labor details in those years that I can't remember them all. One of the most frequent duties was to sort the city garbage dump. The job was a big one and we were usually excused from school for the day. We had to sort the trash into piles of paper or leather or scrap steel, etc., which were in turn reprocessed for further manufacture. Another frequent detail was cleaning the streets of used paper and other litter. Each student was given a stick with a nail at one end for spearing and a paper bag for collection. After a day of this type of labor detail, I suffered from a backache. When the school collected all our full bags, it would turn them over to the factory for making new paper to ease the paper shortage.

Usually on these paper-collection details we were merely told at the beginning of school that we were assigned to pick up litter near a certain location. On some occasions the work was announced in a less direct way. Once, on Memorial Day, when many people visit relatives at the cemeteries, our class was scheduled to pay tribute at a soldiers' graveyard. Everyone wore somber clothes and made some flowers from colored paper. I wore my dark-blue blouse and pants and white socks and shoes. We all gathered at the school early in the morning and boarded a bus for a long ride. We then walked for an hour until we reached the graveyard.

There the teacher read a ceremony commemorating the deeds of the dead from the war against the Kuomintang. After the ceremonies were over, we were exhausted from our trip and thought we were going to return home. But the teacher called a discussion meeting right there at the cemetery. The subject: "What action can you students take to commemorate these soldiers' blood?" The teacher looked at us and continued, "All these brave men have bled. Whom did they bleed for? They bled for us. What can we do today to repay them? What can we do today to make their sacrifices meaningful?"

We were all bewildered and surprised at this sudden discussion, and waited for the teacher to give us some sign of what we could do. He then replied to his own question and spoke of the shortage of paper in Tientsin, and announced a labor detail to collect used paper as repayment for the soldiers.

As on other occasions, I knew that the purpose of the discussion was to get us to pick up waste papers. The soldiers were merely an excuse. But we students all echoed the teacher's suggestion anxiously and walked back to the bus. When we returned to school, we picked up our sticks and bags to search out more waste paper around the area. I didn't get home until after dark, totally exhausted.

Every year at the beginning of summer, we were asked to catch flies. There was never a set quota for each student, but we all knew what would be a creditable amount for the day. In the beginning there were always enough flies to catch, but after several weeks the number of flies would diminish and I soon found myself devoting more and more time to catching flies and less and less time to homework. If the teacher saw that we were losing interest in catching flies, he would give us a pep talk, advising us to think of each fly as a capitalist or as Eisenhower. Every time we swatted a fly, we were killing another of our country's enemies.

During these antipestilence campaigns, our class often went together on Sunday to the riverbank to scare away the sparrows, who were robbing the fields. Some of my friends brought their harmonicas and played songs throughout the day while we sang along and kept accompaniment with our cans of pebbles. The sounds we made frightened the sparrows and most of them flew away. A few dropped dead from exhaustion within our sight. Like many school activities, it was fun for a while, but after that merely boring and tiring. The noise from the shakers almost drove me crazy by the end of the day. On one of these trips to the riverbank, one ambitious student climbed up a tree to scare some birds, lost his balance, fell and broke his leg.

Another frequent labor detail in the city was the construction of a road or a building. We girls were generally assigned to pass building materials such as bricks or cinder blocks along the long line of classmates to the building site. Our work day was eight hours long and we were called into service often, from one day up to three weeks at a time. The work was monotonous and exhausting, but we seldom talked to our neighbors because we were afraid of being branded as loafers. We just passed the heavy bricks endlessly throughout the day. I rarely saw what we were building because we were not allowed to wander from our designated spot on the human conveyor belt.

During these years I was assigned to many such construction projects, but Tientsin's appearance did not seem to change a great deal. There were many roads and buildings started, but they were seldom completed—I suppose there were not enough materials for each job.

In addition to these activities within the city, our class had many assignments on the farms. I never knew when we would go to the country, for we were not told until after we reached school. Sometimes during the day the teacher would announce *lao dung* in the countryside and tell us all to go home and pack and meet later that day or the next morning. If the assignment was a short one, about three days, I took nothing along, not even a toothbrush—only a quilted blanket if it was wintertime. The walks to the farms were often quite long and the light load made the trip easier. For longer periods, I brought a toothbrush, toothpaste, an enamel drinking cup, a blanket and a change of clothing.

I went to approximately ten farms, some more than once, covering a radius of about twenty-five miles from Tienstin. We would stay anywhere from three days to more than a month.

The dormitories varied from farm to farm, with from five to a hundred sleeping in a room. We either slept on the floor—usually two under a blanket to keep warm—or on a *kang*, a northern-style bed, which was a brick slab extending out from the wall; this could hold fifteen of us.

On the farm our day began around five-thirty or six o'clock, depending on the season. We washed up at a riverbank or well. In the winter, we often had to queue up for a half hour to get hot water. After washing, we lined up for breakfast, generally the same corn-husk muffins or corn-flour gruel. We exchanged our coupon for our share, sat on the ground with friends, and ate.

Breakfast over, we were given some tools, usually shovels, hoes or baskets, for which we were responsible and which we kept in our living quarters. We walked from one-half to two miles to reach our work area, where we received instructions from a farmer or a teacher, who also worked along with us.

I am an expert at these duties now, but I remember the first time I harvested. I stood in the rice paddies, bent over with my legs wide apart, grabbing the green sprouts with my left hand and cutting with the sickle in my right hand. It looked simple when the farmer demonstrated, but I gashed my left leg many times before I got used to it. On these harvesting days, I would start the day standing upright, but as the hours wore on I grew more and more tired until I finally dropped in the mud and worked from a sitting position. As I sat in the paddies, I would look up every two or three minutes, hoping to see the food wagon, with its two corn-husk muffins and an hour of rest.

I was never so hungry or thirsty as I was on the farm. For hunger I could give up more food coupons and eat more at meals, but for thirst there was no relief out on the fields. We all drank from the murky river or rain puddles even though we knew we might get very sick from the unclean water.

On these assignments to the farms, I always suffered, either from hunger or from thirst or from exhaustion. The weather in the country seemed to be either furnace hot or icy cold. Even in the more moderate months, the temperature would drop twenty degrees at sunset. Despite these hardships, I had to be enthusiastic and alert to all my duties, because at the end of each day's work there was a student meeting. At these nightly discussions we were to criticize and evaluate each other's efforts during that day. Although we did not receive grades for *lao dung*, the remarks made by fellow students were recorded and included in our "personal files" at school. Such remarks often had greater effect on our futures than our marks in mathematics or literature.

As the school year progressed, I learned that campaigns and labor details and political discussions were inseparable from student life. But I had managed to make the best of the situation by doing my work, by receiving special favors from my teacher superintendent, by getting aid from the boys, who often helped me with heavier duties, and by keeping silent whenever possible during discussions. Thus I had no idea when the poster campaign started that I would be a victim of political criticism. It was during the campaign to "Give Your Heart to the Party" that I came under direct and personal censure.

During a Wednesday political discussion, the teacher told us about the new campaign and explained that we should tell each other openly of our grievances and thus gain a better understanding and establish a better relationship between students, teachers, families, comrades and the party. He elaborated, "As each coin has two sides, so everyone has good and bad qualities. No one on earth is perfect and thus none of us is exempt from constructive criticism from his comrades."

We discussed this new campaign further and it did make sense. We were to carry out the purpose of this campaign by writing our criticisms and displaying them on the school walls for everyone to see. Immediately I took the opportunity to post a complaint about my music teacher. With my brush pen I wrote in bold letters on an old newspaper: "Who is unreasonable? The music teacher is unreasonable and should be criticized." The poster was then tacked up on the wall near his classroom along with the many others written by my classmates. This music teacher soon had enough posters to bind into a book. We disliked him because he was unreasonable in his demands and often embarrassed students who tried hard but just could not sing. During one class a big, husky twenty-year-old farm boy unintentionally sang the wrong tune and was severely reprimanded by this teacher.

I also tacked up notices against teachers who did not explain their lessons clearly, and I soon noticed that they took better care to prepare their classes. As a result of the poster campaign, many such constructive changes were brought about by both students and teachers. Everyone wanted to save face and therefore did his best to meet the criticisms.

The school was soon plastered full of newspaper posters. Not a single wall in classrooms and halls was free from homemade signs. Often we had to put our new signs on top of the old because there was no space left. All these signs were made and tacked up by the students; our teachers posted their signs in the faculty rooms, out of the sight of their pupils.

The campaign became a competition, and by the end of the first month we had nothing more to say. We then either borrowed each other's complaints or manufactured petty offenses.

Most of the students confined their criticisms to one another or to the teachers, but in our school there were about eight students who attacked the government itself. They broke windows in the school and wrote many posters with anti-Communist slogans. They were expelled and never readmitted elsewhere. I don't think these boys were really antigovernment, but merely ruffians who wanted to stir up trouble and attain notoriety. They were all about thirteen or fourteen and their leader, known as The Crazy One, was a most unpopular boy at school. He was boastful and loud and complained wildly against the government during this campaign. I secretly agreed with some of his criticisms but hated him so much that I paid no attention to him. Many thought he was quite insane. I guess they were right, because sometime after the poster campaign he jumped out of a school window, shouting, "I die for a free China."

"Giving Your Heart to the Party" was also an active campaign throughout our entire city. Even in homes, daughters and sons were tacking up notices on their parents' bed—some jokingly, but many seriously. The second daughter of Aunt Number Nine was one of the serious ones, and she brought tragedy to her family. As a student at Peking University, she was very ambitious and anxious to be approved for membership in the Communist Youth League. While her application was still being considered by the Committee, she decided to help her case by reporting on her father. There was nothing in her father's background worth mentioning, so she decided to make up a story. She told the party that her father was a member of the Kuomintang and had accused many innocent people before the liberation. As a result, the authorities immediately started an investigation.

Uncle Number Nine was as devoted to his family as was his loving wife and when he discovered what his own daughter had done, he died—they say of a broken heart. Because his mother was over ninety, Aunt Number Nine never told her of his death but pretended to the old woman that he had a new job many miles away.

In this political campaign, even Mama posted "big news" against the government. She asked why her "lover" ("husband" is not acceptable in Communist vocabulary) was detained for questioning seven nights and days during the Five-Anti Campaign without word to his family.

This first poster campaign flourished for about two months, and then faded away. Throughout the following years, it was periodically revived and it was a common sight to see these newspaper posters around the school. During these campaigns I received my fair share of criticism, mostly against my stubborn nature or my pride. But I took all such notices in stride.

It was not until 1960, when the school first started serving dog meat at lunch, that I was bitterly attacked. The food situation was growing worse and even our laboratory animals—birds, frogs, etc.—were taken into the kitchen after we finished dissecting them in biology. No matter how hungry I was, I just couldn't eat dog meat; the first time I saw it on my lunch plate I recalled Faithful, our neighbor's dog.

Faithful was almost a child to the Yuehs because their own children had left China many years earlier to live abroad. I often chatted with them. They were quite elderly now and enjoyed my foolish ways. One Sunday I was returning from the movies and planned to stop by and tell them about the show, when I saw two men chasing Faithful around the street. One finally caught the small brown dog by his collar and flung the animal against the brick wall of the house. The wall became splattered with red, and the man picked up the limp flesh and carried it down the street. It was only then that I heard old Mrs. Yueh crying for her dear pet. This memory prevented me from obeying the orders to eat dog meat at school.

One morning, a huge poster with my name and my offense glared at me from the classroom wall. A boy named Kao had posted it. Soon other posters followed this example and my name was on the school bulletin board with a line of criticism from every student and every teacher. After this humiliation, I knew that I must never be accused of a misdeed again. But I never did eat dog meat.

During this period of open criticism, I never thought that many who were officially encouraged to speak out would later regret their openness. My history teacher, who was fat and wore glasses, spoke against some of the government policies of censorship during the period the government asked for criticism; later, during the anti-Rightist campaign which followed, he was accused of being a counterrevolutionary on the evidence of his earlier criticisms. He never returned to teach and years after I saw him driving a bus. Another teacher, who came from Peking with many academic honors to teach geography, was demoted to janitor for the boys' room.

My cousin went to engineering college in Shanghai. During the poster campaign in his school, he wrote signs daily objecting to the transfer of his school to a remote province. He must have objected too strongly, because after graduation as an engineer he was assigned to counting ration coupons at a store in remote western China at fifteen yuan per month, while all his classmates received the usual college-graduate salary of forty-two yuan per month.

From neighborhood college students I learned that Peking University students who had criticized the government in the poster campaign were now refused food in the school cafeterias, and when they went off campus to eat, they were not readmitted to the school grounds. Many others who spoke out became known as rightist sympathizers and were refused services at stores even though they had money and coupons.

After participating in the many political campaigns during the eighth and ninth grades and witnessing their consequences, I knew I had to be always watchful of my words and conduct in and out of school. I knew I must say and do just enough to satisfy my political obligations, but never so much as to attract attention. I believed myself clever enough to avoid future political criticism by playing the role of a good student who participated in all campaigns without being labeled an impatient leftist or a backward rightist.

I couldn't explain in words how I knew what to do to keep within the safe areas of a political campaign. I understood instinctively how far I should criticize and how much to keep inside me. I don't believe this sense can be taught, but it is something one learns through experience.

At fourteen I decided upon a plan and a course for the future. I was going to work hard for a good academic record and an inconspicuous political file so that I would be eligible for medical studies. Like so many students, I thought being a doctor a particularly good occupation. I had no romantic dreams about medicine, the way I had had about the stage and acting, but I could see that as a doctor I would be assured of a stable job and a good status in society.

But all these plans were made without foreseeing the implications of the policies of the Great Leap Forward.

The purpose of this campaign, which started in 1958, was for China to make the big leap from agricultural backwardness to modern industrialization by concentrating "twenty years' progress in a single day." The aim was to boost production 100 per cent, lay thousands of miles of railroads, build more factories, manufacture more trucks and tractors, expand trade so that China would surpass Great Britain in fifteen years. Everyone, man, woman and child, was to devote himself to sustained effort and sacrifice to build this new and modern China.

As a result of the Great Leap Forward, work activities in the city and the countryside were increased and many changes resulted. With the building of new factories, more workers were needed and a campaign to "Allow Women to Work" was started. The newspapers shouted equality for the women and freedom from the home and the kitchen. Some women wanted to work and were happy about the new opportunities. Many others went to work for fear of criticism. It didn't make sense for them to work for a salary which just covered the expenses of putting their children in nurseries. They preferred to stay home and take care of their own. While no one spoke out, the dissatisfaction with this phase of the campaign was obvious.

The biggest fear was of working on the farms. Many newspaper articles were written by citizens who demanded their rights to go work on the farms, but I did not believe them. Their protests sounded too pious, especially the one signed by several retired elderly people, who cried out to be allowed to return to work in the fields for their country rather than stay at home. I couldn't believe that these people would leave their homes to work at the bitter rural tasks.

Yet, during the height of the return-to-the-countryside campaign, I saw many trucks filled with people heading for the farms. On these trucks were huge red banners proudly announcing the riders to be volunteers for farm duty.

On the other hand, my neighbor Mrs. Lee, who was rather a nervous and unhappy woman by nature, lived in perpetual fear of being sent away from her family to the farms. Many volunteers were asked to stay in the country for as long as three years. Mousy, fretful Mrs. Lee often came to cry on Mama's shoulders about her fears. Everyone in the block knew how high-strung she was.

One day Mrs. Lee committed suicide. She hanged herself from the door beam between the two rooms of her apartment while her two young sons were sleeping. When one son awoke, he screamed and grabbed for his brother. Their mother's body blocked the doorway. They couldn't move and sat there sobbing. The neighbors heard some noise but thought that Mrs. Lee was punishing her sons again. No one came to the door. The two sat huddled together at the far end of their bed, too weary to continue yelling and too frightened to run. They sat and cried for a day. Finally, the ten-year-old worked up his courage and pried apart the stiffened legs of his dead mother, permitting the small brother to crawl through and out of the room for help.

News of such tragedies and my own experience in school made me naturally skeptical of politics and government campaigns. It seemed that though I had to spend many hours a week listening to lectures on Communism, all speeches said the same thing. Every lecture could be reduced to a call for more work and personal sacrifice for China and the benefit of the people. Whether we swatted flies or posted big news or carried fertilizer or sorted the city dump, we were honored with the opportunity to build our country. I only wished to be so honored less and less, but when everyone contributed their time and muscles, I could not stand alone and refuse. I simply did what I had to, no more and no less.

Despite my disappointment at the political events that changed my carefree school days to long and hard days of physical labor, I was very enthusiastic about the government's program of free education. For it was my only path to a good future. I worked hard throughout junior high school and received good grades in all my subjects, especially in politics classes, where I maintained an average of ninety-eight. I wanted to be appointed to medical studies after graduation from ninth grade. As the time drew near for the final examinations which would determine our future assignments, I studied long hours into the night. Sometimes I fell asleep over my books and was awakened by bats flying through the open window.

The examination consisted of four parts: politics, including current events and the theories of Marx and Lenin; algebra and geometry; Chinese literature; physics and chemistry. We were given two hours for each section. Although I was prepared for the examinations, I was not very confident because I knew the recommendation of my political teacher would have great influence on my future assignment and I did not like or get along with Teacher Wang. He was short, skinny and hairy, with thick black eyebrows that hovered over his eyes like the hands of a clock at eight-twenty. He loved to brag, especially about his political future. He was certain that his application for party membership would soon be signed, for he had the intelligence and the loyalty and the good deeds to merit swift approval. However, his application was never accepted while I was still in school. I so hated his arrogance and manner that I had nicknamed him Long Nose Hairs for obvious reasons. One day he had overheard me referring to him by this name, and ever since I feared for my chances of being approved for medical school.

But after the examinations were over, I returned home feeling I had done quite well. I then waited anxiously for a letter from the authorities about my assignment. After a few days, the letter arrived. My score was quite high—320 out of 400 points. But I was not assigned to medical studies, nor even to high school. I was to go to a school for elementary teachers. I couldn't believe it; there must have been a mistake. But the words on the letter could not be erased. I cried that entire day, and when Mama and Papa returned home, I poured out my disappointment to them for the first time in many years. Mama and Papa were helpless to alter an official decision, and could only suggest that I go to talk to the people at the Education Bureau.

The next morning I walked to the Bureau. When I was shown to the appropriate official, I pleaded with him to reconsider my case. "I have many reasons for wanting to go on to college. I am the youngest in my class and would only be seventeen when I graduate from teachers' school and thus much too inexperienced to be a teacher. Most of my students would probably be older than I. I would still be a child. My family is willing to have me go on to school. They do not need the money so badly as some other parents, whose children have to go to work to help support them. And I am the only child in the family; my parents do not have college degrees and have wished all their lives that I might be given a chance for a higher education."

The man was unmoved and lectured me in return.

"Your wishes should be the wishes of China. You should do what is best for the benefit of the people. China now needs teachers for the Great Leap Forward, and you are assigned to be one of them. You have been given a chance to contribute to the country's welfare. It's a great honor; don't be ungrateful."

I was then dismissed. At fourteen my life was fixed. I was to be an elementary-school teacher in three years and earn thirty-two yuan per month for the rest of my days. I would not have to wonder and plan for my future ever again.

Chapter Five

My future had been decided, but I knew better than to brood about something that I could never change. Besides, I was preoccupied by the increasing difficulty of day-to-day problems and had little energy, time or inclination to dwell upon what might have been. Each day was filled with strenuous activity and what precious time I had to myself each week I saved for the pleasant company of friends or for the movies.

The big change in our daily activities was the result of tighter ration controls. The ration system had been a part of life as long as I could remember, but when I was younger we had more coupon tickets than we could use and the majority of goods was not restricted. By 1959, however, almost everything we ate or wore or used cost both money and coupons. In addition, some articles demanded trade-ins. For example, toothpaste cost money, coupons and an empty tube. Pens were exchanged for the worn-out one only.

With the growing scarcity of goods, I became more and more skeptical of the government's promises of higher standards of living and the advances that were being accomplished under the Great Leap Forward. I could only judge the country's progress by my daily experience on food queues. And it seemed that Tientsin had less and less instead of more and more.

I first began to distrust government promises after the announcement that under no circumstances would cotton undershirts ever be rationed. Mama had heard a rumor that they would soon be controlled and sent me to the store to buy several. I had intended to do so, but because the newspapers announced that the rumor was completely false and that no one needed to hoard cotton undershirts, I did not buy them. Only three weeks later they were rationed. From then on I didn't believe everything I read in the newspapers.

Thus, while the papers talked about China's progress, I suspected otherwise, because the ration system became increasingly complex and tight. The system was so complicated that even Mama and Papa did not understand it; only I, who did the daily shopping, was able to keep up with all its changes.

The government issued many types of ration coupons. The most basic type was issued by the Street Council once a year, at New Year's, to every family in its district. Each household received four books of twelve pages (one to a month) each, for: (1) industrial goods such as light bulbs, thread; (2) secondary foods such as marmalade, fish, yeast, sometimes fruit; (3) staples such as grain, rice or noodles; (4) fuel, consisting of coal and firewood. No one could be assured of any item because the amount was not guaranteed; the total amount and individual portions rationed would constantly change, depending on the supply.

The second type of ration book given to every family by the Street Council was the vegetable book, but this was issued by the season instead of by the year. Here, too, the actual amount one could buy with a ticket fluctuated with the supply. Usually our family of three could obtain from nine to eighteen ounces per day.

The third ration book, issued individually to each citizen once a month, included meat, soap, cloth. However, some months we did not have any meat. And beginning in 1960 we received only two bars of soap and two feet seven inches of cloth per year. While these books were given to everyone, they still did not ensure a minimum amount, because the tickets could redeem only what was released by the government on a day-to-day basis.

The fourth type of rationing comprised the coupons issued to workers only. Each salaried worker who earned forty yuan or less was entitled each month to four industrial and four secondary food coupons; for those who earned more than this, an extra coupon of both categories was added for each increment of ten yuan.

The number of coupons needed to purchase a product varied from day to day. For example, I noticed one Monday that a radio cost thirty-two coupons and the next day the price had jumped to sixty-five coupons.

In addition to these controls, many valuable products, such as yarn or sleeping mats, could only be secured through winning a factory raffle.

For the very few who were extremely wealthy, there were the high-class products, which did not call for coupons or tickets but whose prices were prohibitive to practically all citizens. For example, a box of high-quality cookies cost twenty-five yuan; a bicycle, 750 yuan; a scoop of ice cream, eighty cents; a blouse, thirty yuan.

Because of this tight ration system, every day except Sunday began for me at three in the morning. When my alarm rang at that early hour, I would stumble out of bed and grope in the dark for my shoes and jacket and the food basket. I tried to leave them within easy reach the night before because I didn't want to turn on the overhead bulb and really be awakened. Then I sought my way down the dark stairs by leaning my shoulder against the wall. The outside air was brisk, but I was still more or less sleepwalking as I made my way down the block to find the queue of empty baskets. I then left my basket in line, anchored down by a huge rock to discourage anyone from stealing it. Several times a thief did remove the rock and run away with my basket, but in the handicraft sessions of *lao dung* I had learned how to weave such baskets and was able to replace the few that were taken. With the skies still dark, I returned to bed for another two and a half hours.

At about six, the huge iron cart with our daily vegetable rations normally appeared on our block. Sometimes I would time it just right and run to help the man pull his load in return for first turn at the market. But usually I waited in line behind my neighbors. It was not a pleasant group of people—everyone still grouchy from sleep, anxious to get their share and hurry home for breakfast and work. Also, as the food supply grew smaller and smaller, and as our diet consisted inevitably of dried beans or sweet potatoes, we all suffered from stomach growls and other involuntary body sounds. At first I had difficulty suppressing giggles of embarrassment whenever the woman in front or in back interrupted the silence. But soon I grew so accustomed to the bodily noises that I didn't even blush.

While thus waiting on the vegetable queue, I played a game with myself. I tried to guess what the man was selling that day; was it spinach or onions or cabbage—or maybe, just maybe, it was chestnuts. Chestnuts—how I craved chestnuts. I remembered the many times I used to buy a sizable bag of them for mere pennies on the way home from grammar school; how crisp and sweet they were. But that had been many years ago, and the last time the man had chestnuts to sell was at New Year's, and each buyer was rationed four. How angry I was when I discovered that two out of my four were rotten.

I wasn't the only one who played this guessing

game. Many others diverted themselves this way, because we all spent many hours a day just waiting in queues. Whenever we spotted a line of people in the street, we would automatically get on it. No matter what was being sold, we could use it. Only once did I learn of an exception to this rule. My neighbor down the block got on the tail of a very long queue one day and waited almost three hours before reaching her turn. The salesman then asked, "What measurements?"

Bewildered, she replied, "What measurements do you need?"

"Comrade, don't you even know what you have been waiting to buy?"

"No, but it doesn't matter. Whatever it is, I am sure I need it."

The man smiled. "OK, OK, but I will still have to have somebody's measurements for the coffin."

I repeated this incident many times to friends and we would all laugh, for we recognized the humor in our daily routine.

After I purchased the family vegetables each morning, which varied from two ounces to one-half pound of whatever was available that day, I rushed home to drop off the materials for our dinner and picked up my books to catch the bus for school. The old buses of Tientsin were always tightly packed and some mornings I stood in line while several passed before one would pick me up. I used to comply with the campaign for courtesy to mothers carrying babies or to families of soldiers who showed the government paper giving them the privilege to go to the head of any line. But no more; too often was I stranded without a ride and too many mornings did the vegetable cart run out of supplies before my turn. So now I and everyone else refused to be gallant.

I rode the bus for about three-quarters of an hour and, after getting off, walked another twenty minutes before reaching school. By then I was starved for my breakfast of one corn-husk pancake, which I could buy at school for three cents.

Classes began at eight and lunch was at noon. When I was in grammar school, I used to bring my lunch, but now there was not much food left over at home, and we all ate in school. Lunch was always the same two corn-husk muffins, a vegetable, and soy-bean sauce in hot water. On some days there was not enough soy sauce, and a little salt or raw sugar was substituted. In the summer heat we took a nap after lunch at our desk or listened to a classmate read articles selected by the teacher from the daily newspaper.

Then three more classes and school was out at four. If I did not have labor-service activities, I often practiced on the school piano or joined some friends in singing some songs. Several times our class produced original plays and I always took part. The students did the entire production from writing the script and composing the songs to playing the roles. I remember one particular comedy show, which we hoped to enter in a district competition. We all worked very hard and after the performance were very pleased and proud. However, the next day, our political teacher held a criticism session. She said that we only paid attention to the melody and not to the lyrics. We all sang beautifully, but we talked about romance and other unimportant matters. "Love is of no use." We should have sung about the glories of socialism or the revolution. She cautioned us to work more on the libretto and less on the melodies next time.

I always wanted a part in every production even though it meant my reaching the house too late to have supper ready on the table for Mama and Papa. Generally I got home about five-thirty and began immediately to prepare the dinner. After I washed the vegetables, I lugged our metal stove carefully, one side step at a time, down the stairs to the yard. Then I fed the stove coal and kindling, and nursed it until it was burning steadily.

Papa and Mama returned home around six-thirty and we ate at seven. No one talked much at the table, because it is impolite. After our short meal, I collected the dishes and washed them in the community kitchen on the first floor, while Papa listened to the radio and Mama read the newspaper. After my chores, I did homework and was in bed by nine. This was my routine pattern every day except Sunday.

On Sundays I awoke about six to get an early start so that I would finish my chores in time to go to the movies. Since there was little time during the week to do anything besides cooking and shopping, there was much for me to do on Sundays. I usually started with the family wash—all our clothing, towels and sheets, done in the tub with a wooden scrub board and water that had been filtered through the ashes of seaweed to produce a primitive lye. Soap was too valuable for use in the laundry. Mama would offer to help, but I never accepted. I remembered that everything had still been soiled the last time she did the laundry and had to be scrubbed again. After I finished, I hung the wash in our yard. Then I chipped enough coal for the rest of the week, mended torn clothing, washed the floors of both rooms, and did anything else around the house that was needed.

When I completed everything, I went to the movies with friends. This was what I liked to do most of all; I could watch movies every afternoon of the week and never tire of them. Even when the same picture played several weeks in all the theaters, I would see it two or three or even four times. Although there were about twenty-five theaters in town, movie tickets were at a premium. The cost of a ticket was quite reasonable—only fifteen cents for students— but everyone loved the movies and long lines formed before each showing. Therefore we girls often asked the boys to bicycle ahead and buy our tickets for us.

I loved the foreign pictures most. I don't think that Chinese make good actors and actresses, and most Chinese movies revolved around the same type of political stories about farmers or steelworkers or the revolution. I preferred the classical stories and costume pictures from Russia or other European countries; my favorites were *Twelfth Night* and *Othello* from Russia and *The Red Shoes* from England.

Mama and Papa liked the movies too, but since Papa's day off was Wednesday and did not coincide with ours, he generally went by himself. Mama often wanted to accompany me to the movies, but I tried to avoid it. She always looked sloppy, her collar unbuttoned, her clothing wrinkled and unkempt. But worst of all, she refused to wear a brassiere. She thought they were terribly uncomfortable and no matter how I begged her, she wouldn't wear one. I didn't want to be seen walking beside her.

I suppose I was too hard on her, because she was always suffering from glandular problems. The doctors prescribed numerous medicines but none seemed to help. Periodically her five-foot body puffed up like a huge balloon, and toward the end of each day she would grow more and more tired. She slept as much as she could. Even though I knew Mama was a victim of her illness, it was hard to be sympathetic; there were months when all I could remember about her was that she slept. It seemed to me that she didn't even make an effort to keep awake and do things like other people. Sometimes she herself criticized her lack of self-discipline and vowed to change. But she never kept any of her promises, and I told myself that she was just plain lazy.

If Mama was lazy, she at least felt guilty about it. Not Papa. He believed we owed him his comfort. When he came home at night, he would take off his coat and sit waiting to be served. He never performed even the smallest chore around the house. One evening I was preparing supper in the yard and left the rice cooking while I went to chop the vegetables in the community kitchen. Mama was busy feeding the chickens and Papa sat in his chair near the stove reading the newspaper. When Mama noticed the rice burning, she immediately screamed at me for being careless. Papa could easily have averted the disaster merely by rising from his chair near the stove and taking the pot off.

For someone who sang loud praises of socialism and the work needed to be done for China, Papa loved his luxuries and comforts more than anyone else. Many a night Mama and I took turns scratching his feet while he listened contentedly to a ball game on the radio. He was first to reprimand me for a bourgeois love of luxuries if I wanted an extra few pennies for a piece of candy, but it never occurred to him that he was being inconsistent when he bought on the black market or when he persuaded friends in Hong Kong to send him spoonfuls of coffee in their letters. With one breath he praised the greatness of Chairman Mao, and with the next he complained about wearing an old suit.

For these reasons, there was little conversation around the house, and almost every night after dinner, Mama would fall asleep, Papa would turn to the radio or newspaper, and I would go to my room. They never asked me about school, except at report-card time. If I did badly, they scolded me, but never once did they offer to talk it over or to help me with my homework. The three of us just didn't have anything to say to each other.

As the years passed it seemed that the few times that Mama and Papa talked, it led inevitably to a fight, always about something very small. Mama's ill health made her irritable, and she usually started the arguments. I became used to their squabbling and never even listened. Only on one occasion was I frightened. It was Mama's birthday and she wanted to go out dancing. The day before, after a fierce argument, Papa had reluctantly promised to take her. He didn't like to go out with Mama in public because many people quite naturally thought he was her father. But that night, he deliberately stayed out after work and didn't come home until ten, much too late to go dancing. Mama was furious and the two fought for hours, screaming at each other. Even upstairs I could hear every accusation. I was ashamed, for I knew the neighbors could also hear Mama's language, which was the most vulgar street slang. She was crazy with anger, called him a shriveled old man, and even demanded a divorce. After several hours, I finally fell asleep during the fight.

For many days they did not exchange a word, but finally everything returned to normal and we all went on as before.

Because of the situation at home, I looked more and more to my friends for pleasant company and fun. All my good friends from junior high except Mah were assigned to the teachers' school. I still recall vividly the day I accompanied her to the Student Health Center for our annual checkup. When she came out of the examining room, she quietly told me that the doctor had discovered a severe case of tuberculosis. Silently we walked back to the classroom. Mah never complained or mentioned her condition again, but she wore a white cloth hospital mask to school thereafter. When we received our assignments at the end of ninth grade, Mah was given a job as a clerk. I seldom saw her again, but we exchanged many letters. I even wrote her a poem in my New Year's card.

You are most brave,
Like an eagle soaring in a cloudless sky.
The wind blows and all return to their
    nests,
But you continue into the wind.
The thunder clamors;
You challenge it with your song.
The lightning dances;
You never swerve from your flight.

Big Nose, however, was going to be a teacher like myself, and we continued to see each other at school. By now he and I had a special relationship and had adopted each other as brother and sister. Once he had had a real sister, but she died at the age of four. Big Nose had been with her at the hospital when she cried out, "Elder brother, elder brother, I don't want to die. I don't want to die." He smoothed her brow and tried to comfort her. He fainted when he realized that she was already dead. Since then, he carried this tragedy in his heart, and grew up with a special sensitivity for family and home life. He was always helpful, and could cook and sew. When his father was ill, Big Nose often refused to eat and saved his share for him. I admired his devotion; he thought I resembled his lost sister. Thus we adopted each other. Such a warm relationship between boy and girl at our age was very unusual.

Because we were so close, I could speak to him more frankly than to other friends, and I even lectured him at times. Once I caught him eating some of the candies we were assigned to wrap in the factory. I sought him out privately and said, "You can buy a piece of candy for two cents, but for two cents you can never buy your self-respect or a good reputation. Please, don't steal any more candies." He looked sheepish, laughed, and never ate any more candies that he did not buy. Another time I found him smoking horse-manure cigarettes; many boys smoked these homemade cigarettes because they could not get tobacco. I told him of my disapproval and, although I was younger, he listened to my plea and never smoked again.

Big Nose enjoyed a reputation for being clever and talented, but he never studied. He was more interested in playing the piano, learning new songs or entertaining us with an imitation. His wit was sharp and always won him applause. He was the one who nicknamed me Chopping Board because I was only five feet tall. Everyone at school admired his acting talents and believed that he would surely go to acting school. Big Nose even persuaded his parents to give him their permission. It wasn't easy because his mother, who was quite "progressive," frowned upon the profession and had actually locked his elder brother in the house, a few years before, to keep him from enrolling in the theater. Big Nose was always set on being an actor and did everything to prepare himself. He was in all the school plays and exercised his voice daily. In fact, he refused to wear his much-needed glasses because he believed no actor would wear them.

This preparation was in vain; he too was assigned to be a teacher.

Unlike Big Nose, who was not interested in good grades, my good friend Lee studied late into each night, only to get up and start all over again. She was pretty, intelligent and always first in our class. She was also a good athlete; her time on the 800-meter run was the record for our school. But after this success in seventh grade, she retired from any further athletic competition. Lee did not want to have a reputation in athletics for fear the school would assign her to be a physical-èducation teacher. She also shied away from taking official jobs in school. Because she was so bright, teachers often asked her to be class assistant. These honors she accepted reluctantly, since she would rather have spent the time studying and ensuring her chance to go to college.

We were very good friends and I affectionately called her Skinny Monkey, because she was so thin, not because she resembled a monkey. In fact, Lee was one of the prettiest girls in school—tall, with beautiful black eyes, a high forehead, a sweet mouth. She was a truly lovely person and I told her so in my poem:

Peacocks sing duets with you.
You are the young lotus blossoming above a
  crystal-blue lake.

Although she was well ahead of everyone in class, Lee still studied night and day. Often the first words she would say to me when we met would be about a homework problem. But despite her intelligence and hard work, she was absentminded and had a reputation for being accident-prone. When she first started elementary school, she was struck by a soy-sauce cart two days in a row. A few years later she swallowed a whistle. The doctors ordered her to go on a diet of bananas, and her poor mother had to search for the whistle. There were numerous stories about her mishaps, but the one I remember best of all is the time we marched in a parade together. The streets were crowded and banners flew everywhere; it was exciting and we enjoyed the day off from school. But somehow during the march, Skinny Monkey lost both her shoes and had to go home barefoot.

Although Skinny Monkey was naturally shy and I was always talkative, we were very close. Her house was only a block from mine and we went to school together every morning. We always seemed to have a lot to tell each other, and often walked each other home many times from her door to mine and back before we finally parted for the night.

The day after I received my letter from school announcing my assignment to teachers' school, Lee came to see me. Her eyes were red and I realized that she had been crying too. I just couldn't believe that she did not get assigned to college-preparatory school, for she had received 396 out of 400 points on the exams. She too was to be a teacher.

If Lee was first in our class, my other good friend, Feng, was always second. Feng was not quite so smart as Lee, but she worked even harder. Her quiet and retiring manner reflected her love of reading and studying. Whenever possible, she quoted from literature rather than make any comment of her own. Although she looked studious, even aloof, she was not so with me. She didn't mind when I decided to call her

94

Chocolate and her brother Sweet Potato because of their dark complexions.

Feng wanted to be a doctor. She gladly would have locked herself in the library for years doing research without coming out, so I tried to pry her from her studies whenever possible. Even during the New Year's holiday she was studying. Finally I persuaded her to go ice skating with me, but she was not at all coordinated and I had to hold her up most of the time. She was purple and I was blue when we reached home that afternoon.

Another time I was successful in getting her away from the books was the Sunday we went swimming at a nearby public pool. For fifteen cents each we could swim for one and a half hours. Neither Chocolate nor I could swim very well, but we enjoyed paddling around the cool waters to escape the heat of summer. After our time was up, I changed quickly into dry clothing and waited for Chocolate. I waited and waited. Finally, after an hour, she emerged from the girls' dressing room with a huge smile. I asked her what had kept her so long. She replied, ''The attendant gave me a small piece of soap for free and I took a long shower. Afterward, I dried myself and got dressed, but when I realized that there was still some soap left, I undressed and decided to wash my hair. No use wasting a chance to shower or a free piece of soap.''

Feng was a good friend for many years and I shall always remember how she and Mah nursed me the first time we were assigned to the farms. For her I wrote this poem:

Like a lofty pine, you stand on a mountain
    top, ever green,
More pleasing and good than
The prettiest of flowers in a porcelain vase.

Unfortunately Feng's studies were not rewarded. She will never be a doctor, for she too was assigned to teachers' school.

We all felt cheated, disappointed and angry when we first learned we were to be elementary-school teachers. But by the time school started in September, we were no longer frustrated and were resigned to our fates. We knew there was nothing we could do to change our assignments and the problems of mere day-to-day existence kept our minds occupied. We seldom talked about the future, for there was nothing to discuss and it was better not to dwell on sadness.

Chapter Six

One morning as I was walking to the bus stop, I noticed many homemade signs tacked on the walls of the buildings that I passed. The signs were all put up by one person, a man named Ho, who had recently arrived in Tientsin from Sian. Apparently some thief had stolen his wallet and Mr. Ho hoped to get back his very important identification papers by publicly addressing the thief through these posters. The posters promised the thief that he could keep all of the two hundred yuan, the coupons and the wallet itself, if only he would return the identification papers. Since he had just arrived from out of town, he had to have these papers to establish his identity and his citizenship. Otherwise he would be a "black" person and therefore unable to work. No work, no coupons; and without coupons he would be unable to buy food or supplies. Also, since the authorities do not recognize any substitute for identity papers, Mr. Ho could fall under suspicion as a Taiwan spy.

The man must really be desperate, I thought, as I passed by his fifth poster. Yet during that year of 1960, almost everyone seemed desperate. The food situation deteriorated to the point where no rations were given for rice or meat that year. We all lived with hunger and anxiety for the future. Hard conditions forced many people in Tientsin to take impulsive, foolish, even dangerous chances to try to cope with the times. I knew some very unlikely people who got into trouble with the authorities during 1960.

The bus driver who took me to school each morning told me of an old woman who tried to cheat someone out of a package and ended up only with trouble. The bus had been coming to its last stop with only a handful of passengers left. As they filed out, the driver noticed a large package in the back and shouted for its owner. No one spoke up immediately, and all looked toward the back of the bus. The driver again asked for the owner. This time an old woman of about seventy spoke up and said that the package belonged to her; she explained that she was getting on in years and that her memory wasn't very good. She then started back toward the rear of the bus, carefully holding on to the backs of the seats to steady her. When she reached the package, she was unable to lift it, almost falling in her attempt to budge the brown-papered parcel. She then called for the help of the driver, who found the package surprisingly heavy. When he had set the package beside the old woman on the street corner, he suddenly realized that if she could not carry the package off the bus, she could not have managed to carry it on. He knew the old woman was lying and asked her to identify the contents. She had nothing to say, only that the package was hers. The bus driver loosened the string around the package and unwrapped the brown paper. Inside were cut-up parts of a dead body. Everyone screamed, and a policeman came to investigate. The old woman squatted down and began to cry and yell, "The package isn't mine. I didn't kill anyone. I just hoped to get whatever was in the package. I thought it might be old papers or rags or other junk. But it isn't mine."

Another old woman down the street, Widow Wang, also got into serious trouble when she tried to obtain some extra money. The widow lived down the hall from a young couple who had recently been married. One morning they were late for work and rushed out of the building without locking their door. When the widow passed down the hall, she noticed her neighbors' door ajar and peeked inside. On the table she saw a magnificent thermos bottle, over a foot tall and with a steel covering. It was the type of thermos bottle that was only available to newlyweds as a wedding present from the state; no other citizens were given the ration coupons necessary to buy such a big bottle. The widow paused in front of the open door; she had had a very hard year and could not resist the temptation of taking the bottle. It would fetch many yuan on the black market. She quickly took the bottle and went several blocks from her home and sat down on the curb with it beside her. She was certain that a customer would soon approach her and offer her a handsome sum. Suddenly, a boy on his bicycle came whizzing around the corner, and before the widow could protect her prize, the boy crashed into the sidewalk and broke it.

The boy knew it was his fault, and offered to pay five yuan. But the widow was not satisfied, for on the black market she could have got at least twenty-five yuan for it. The boy and the old woman haggled—she screaming for full payment, and he claiming that five yuan was enough since she was acting illegally by selling the bottle on the black market. A policeman heard their shouts and asked for an explanation. After he heard both sides of the story, he picked up the broken thermos to inspect its inside. Unscrewing the top, he saw the bottle was jammed full of ration coupons. Peddling articles on the black market was so common in 1960 that the police found it impossible to control; and therefore a majority of citizens bought and sold on the streets without any consequences. However, stealing coupons was a most serious offense. When the widow realized that she was under suspicion for stealing coupons, she immediately confessed to stealing the thermos bottle from her neighbors. Neither her theft nor her selling on the black market was serious. But the young married couple were certain to get the death penalty for stealing ration coupons.

Since stealing ration coupons meant the death penalty and money was useless without necessary coupons, thieves generally stole used clothing or goods. In our neighborhood, someone stole the clothes and shoes from a boy and a girl, killed them and left them naked in the snow, with a note in which the killer identified himself as a Taiwan spy. The police believed that the murderer was trying to make it look like the work of strangers in the neighborhood. Therefore I and everyone else had to copy the killer's note so the police could compare handwritings. I was scared; what if my handwriting happened to resemble his? The police did not show the actual note to me, and thus I couldn't be sure that my writing did not match until the police allowed me to leave.

Although in the cities we suffered greatly from the shortages of 1960, we were still much better off than most of the farmers, who fled with their families from the countryside to the cities. But after many came to Tientsin, the city could offer them nothing. I saw for myself their new urban life.

Near school was a restaurant where the students often went for dinner when special political meetings were held at night. The restaurant was generally crowded, not only with customers but also with filthy farmers' children, looking like greasy soy-sauce bottles. As soon as someone sat down, little rags immediately squatted on the floor beside him. Hungry eyes dominated conversation at the table, and no one could ignore these begging children with scabbed thin bodies, bulging stomachs, shreds of dirty clothing and black feet. Like their farming parents, they were known for their thick skins and shamelessness. They camped in the previously clean railroad station and turned the waiting room into a garbage hole of litter, waste and sleeping bodies. The adults begged in the streets while the children infested the restaurants. At first the restaurants tried shooing them out, but there proved to be too many of them. As soon as one group was out the door, another one would sneak in. No one paid attention to them anymore.

No matter how many times I went to eat at the restaurant, I could not get used to the hungry chants of "Give me a bite, give me a bite," whenever food arrived at the table. The children's monotone voices droned on throughout the meal, and, as soon as someone finished, hands grabbed for the empty bowls and skillful tongues licked them clean inside and out.

The situation on the farms was so serious that the school held a special meeting to discuss Chairman Mao's speech on agriculture. I remembered this speech because it was quite different from the usual praise of socialism and China's progress.

At the meeting, our politial teacher reported that Chairman Mao had said that the people on the farm communes had not progressed enough in socialism to permit the strict interpretation of the "Law of Equality." During the Great Leap Forward and the beginning of the formation of farm communes, Chairman Mao had said that everyone on the communes was entitled to an equal share. As a result, many of the poorer peasants went to the more fortunate ones and demanded a share of their crops on the basis of what Mao had proclaimed. The wealthier farmers had no choice but to share with the poorer ones. Thereafter they worked less hard. As a result, Mao said, they became poor, and the poor became destitute. The Chairman said that this should not be the result of communization and the Law of Equality; therefore it was obvious that the people were not yet ready for putting these ideas into effect. In his speech Mao listed sixty items concerning the life of the farmers and the improvement of their situation. They were to be granted some private plots, which they could cultivate and harvest for their individual use. They were to be given holidays, four monthly for women, two for men.

Mao also admitted some abuses of power by the local party cadres (Kanpus), who used their position to work for personal gain rather than for the benefit of the people. The Kanpus had taken advantage of the fact that party leaders did not live in the countryside and therefore could not monitor their activities. In the sixty items, Mao included the correct code of conduct for these Kanpus.

The government also ran large campaigns to try to relieve the people's complaints. During 1960 everyone needed new clothes to wear but didn't even have enough for patching old garments out of the yearly cloth rations of two feet seven inches. I remember wearing out the seat of the blue pants that I wore to school and having to camouflage the hole by dying my white underpants with blue ink. When the government realized that the people had only old and patched-up clothes to wear, it started the campaign of the glorious patches. Each patch was to symbolize dedication to socialism and the people. After the campaign started, I couldn't have worn good clothing to school even if I had had it; I would have suffered the abuse of the more progressive students, who took pride in wearing more and more glorious patches for China.

The food shortage in Tientsin was getting worse daily, and the government reversed its ban on birth control and began an intensified campaign to hold down the population. During the Great Leap Forward, unrestrained population expansion was one of the means to achieve China's goals. But now the newspapers carried daily information on the methods of birth control, and I was careful to avoid the man at the bus station who eagerly passed out birth-control literature and sold prophylactics to passengers. As a result of this reversal, a doctor at Mama's hospital who had performed abortions was freed from jail and was now considered a great physician. Under the sponsorship of the government, he now lectured as a specialist in abortions at many hospitals throughout the north.

Although I had seen this famous doctor at the hospital where Mama was working, I did not know him as well as I knew some of the other workers, like the dietician, Mrs. Chan. She had been with the hospital for over twenty years and took pride in her work. Whenever I waited for Mama to finish her job, I chatted a few minutes with Mrs. Chan. She impressed me; unlike Mama, she was always neatly dressed, her hair combed and her nails perfect. When I was still in junior high school and wanted to be a doctor, I often asked her many questions about hospital life. Mrs. Chan liked me and encouraged me to go on to medical school. She herself was a college graduate and very proud of it.

The last time I saw Mrs. Chan, I was frightened. I was walking down the hospital corridor when she suddenly appeared and fell upon her knees and kowtowed three times to me. She then jumped up and quickly fled. I was so surprised that I couldn't be sure it was really she. The woman that kowtowed to me barely resembled the dignified and proper dietician of the hospital. When I found Mama, I told her what had happened, and she explained to me Mrs. Chan's sad story.

As the food shortage grew worse and worse, even the meals at the hospital were limited to corn-husk muffins or gruel with some vegetables. This made a dietician's job useless. Everyone ate the same thing every day. At first Mrs. Chan tried to look busy by helping the cook prepare the meals, but it was obvious that the hospital no longer needed her services. One day the hospital director came to see her and said that starting the next day she was to be the information clerk in the lobby. The proud Mrs. Chan was very unhappy; she resented being a clerk and petitioned the hospital for retirement. The authorities did not accept her petition, and she worked as information clerk for several months before people noticed that there was something very peculiar about her behavior. Her neat appearance changed, she spoke only in whispers, and she began to kowtow to anyone she met in the halls.

The authorities were not concerned at first, thinking it was merely a fraud to gain approval for her early retirement. After repeated instances such as the one I had just seen, Mama thought, they must now be convinced of her insanity and would soon let her retire.

Mama's hospital was always overcrowded, and there never seemed to be enough doctors around. The daily queue of patients grew longer and longer until finally they had to institute two lines—one for those with under 102 degrees temperature, and one for those with 102 and over. Fever seemed to be the most prevalent complaint. Many people in school often ran temperatures for weeks and weeks without any relief. The doctors could not find any cure, and the sick continued to suffer from lack of energy.

Since so many people complained of illness, the authorities began a campaign to reduce absenteeism. Anyone who stayed away from work or school needed a signed certificate from a doctor. The doctor at our school was a good friend and liked me. One afternoon at school, I went to see him because of severe monthly cramps. I had expected to be excused from school for the rest of that day, but he gave me a two-day permit and sent word of my illness to my teacher. When my teacher heard that I had received a two-day excuse, she immediately asked two boys to get the stretcher and see me home. She then called the hospital and notified Mama that I was on the way home on a stretcher with a two-day excuse.

When I saw the boys coming with the stretcher, I knew that the teacher must have decided I was very seriously ill because of the unusual two-day excuse. I knew I couldn't explain the friendly act of the school doctor, so I pretended for the boys until they reached the bus stop. I then got off the stretcher and told them to go back to school; I was quite capable of reaching home alone by bus. They left reluctantly.

When I reached home and opened the front door, I found Mama and a doctor from the hospital waiting anxiously for me. She had become alarmed and summoned him when she heard of my two-day excuse. I was embarrassed, but I quickly explained what had happened. I would have laughed at the whole incident but for the fact that Mama and the doctor had gone to much trouble.

Starting that year, whenever I had a chance to chat with fellow students at school, we would inevitably turn to the subject of food. We reminisced about all our favorite dishes or boasted of a recent bargain at the market. I often told a story which made everyone laugh. A few weeks previously, I explained to my friends, I had received a food package from Hong Kong relatives that was wrapped in burlap. I carefully saved the cloth for a pair of pants I was going to have made. Since I loved clothes and there was rarely an opportunity to be stylish, I made a special trip to the tailor to explain to him what I wanted done with the additional burlap. I explained that I wanted two pockets sewn on the blue pants he was making for me. I didn't want the ordinary straight-up-and-down pockets in the front of the pants, but slanted ones over the hips. About a week later, I went to pick up my new pants and discovered to my horror that the old tailor had misunderstood my very unique innovation and patched four pockets onto the pants—two in front and two in back. I was heartbroken. Instead of looking stylish I looked silly.

Only later did I discover that the tailor had done me a great favor. I wore these pants to school, and one day on the way I spotted a farmer selling some of the red-hot peppers that I love so much. Because I had four pockets, I was able to carry home twice as many peppers as usual. I was pleased after all about my new pair of pants.

We all loved to discuss food among ourselves and even the newspapers carried articles about getting the most out of what was available. I remember one news article about frying fish that everyone heeded. The cooking expert reported that fish eyes absorb an undue amount of cooking oil and that if they are removed, much oil can be saved without altering the taste of the fried fish. Although we often complained to one another about being hungry, I seldom heard any student blame the government. The only exceptions were stories passed on to me by close friends, like Big Nose.

He told me he had heard a new version of the old song "Socialism Is Good." At a public toilet in town, through closed doors, he heard someone singing:

> "Socialism is good,
> Socialism is good,
> But it cannot feed my stomach."

He asked, "Who's that?" The singing stopped and feet ran out of the room.

Big Nose told another story, which painted such a perfect picture of the times that I laughed and laughed every time I remembered it. The popular tale is about a man and his wife who lived in a small house in Tientsin. One winter their stove broke down and they tried to buy a new one. They had enough coupons and the money, but so many people needed stoves that winter, they had to wait. Their names were included on the long list and their number would probably come up in three months.

Meanwhile, the fumes from the old stove were strong and one day knocked the wife unconscious. When the husband reached home, he immediately carried his wife to the hospital.

The hospital was jammed full; people with a

variety of ills were lying on thin slabs of wood three layers high in huge rooms. The doctors were overworked and overtired. Nevertheless, the hospital accepted his wife and the man returned home. The woman was put on an empty slab and in a few hours was pronounced dead.

The hospital officials notified the husband, but the husband was working so hard at the factory that he did not have time to claim his wife. He knew it would probably take three months to reach the end of the coffin queue; therefore he gave the hospital permission to lay the body in the ground.

The gravediggers were very busy too and it would take them another three days of digging before they would inter her body. Meanwhile, the woman awoke from her coma and, still dressed in the white paper shroud, began to walk home. Cloth was precious and no longer wasted on the dead.

She arrived at her house by nightfall and knocked on the door, crying, "Open up, husband, I am cold and hungry. Open up immediately." The frightened husband dug his heels into the ground and pushed his back against the locked door, praying that the ghost of his dissatisfied wife could not knock it down. The husband begged, "I am sorry that I did not go to see you at the hospital. The factory has a production quota to meet and I could not ask for a day's absence. Rest in peace, dear wife, and do not haunt me any longer."

The wife shouted back, "I am alive. Let me in,

you big fool. I am alive. I am alive.'' But it was no use: the husband was asleep, exhausted, against the door.

The woman then went to the Census Bureau to claim her food coupons for the month. But the census bureaucrat said, ''You are dead according to the books and therefore are not entitled to any coupons.'' The woman had no more success persuading the census man that she was alive than she had had persuading her husband.

She then went to the police to ask them to force her husband to let her back into their home. The police replied, ''You are dead according to the books and therefore not entitled to any services.''

In despair the woman returned to the hospital graveyard. Fortunately, the diggers had not yet passed her body in line.

This story touched on problems that dwelt on my mind every day. I could not think of tomorrow when my stomach was not full today. Often in that year of 1960 we had two tomatoes along with the usual corn-husk muffins to share among the three of us for dinner. Muffins could no longer satisfy my hunger, for they were dry and contained no oil; they were only corn husks mixed with water and rolled into a ball that was baked until done. Instead of being filled by its bulk, I was curiously more and more hungry.

I longed for more variety. When I worked in the school kitchen, I salvaged the scraps of rotten or dry vegetables thrown on the floor. When I worked on the farms, I gathered wild plants during rest hour. They were bitter, but I was no longer particular. As the year wore on, however, I couldn't even get these bitter plants. Whenever I and my friends would try to pick them, farmers would drive us away, shouting, "Get away from here! If you pick all the wild plants, what do you expect us to eat? Go away! We have to live too."

At home we were living on two to four ounces of vegetables a day and corn-husk muffins at every meal. We longed for noodles, rice or meat, but these had disappeared from our ration quotas for several months at a time. Thus corn-husk flour became our main staple. This flour was merely the ground-up skin of corn kernels whose meat had already been extracted for export as soup to countries such as Albania. What was left was not at all pleasing. Every day I mixed the flour with water and patted the dough with my hands into a ball which was cooked in the stove. No matter how I tried, there was little I could do to disguise the dry and bland taste of the unhealthy-looking yellow muffins, for we only had two ounces each of sugar and salt a month. We all got very tired of this diet, but at school we tried to laugh about the food situation and dubbed these awful muffins "golden towers."

The government in the newspapers and at school also deplored the food crisis. Our teacher had repeatedly told us that the weather in the past three years had been so bad that the farmers could not grow enough cotton or grain for all the Chinese people. He would admit the scarcity of food and clothing, but assured us that tomorrow it would be dawn, a dawn when all our hardships would vanish, a dawn toward which everyone must work. And since we all wanted to see the dawn soon, we must all sustain even more hardships in our daily lives.

One of these additional hardships was the reduction of staples. In the past our Street Council had decided on the amount of staples an individual received each month. Now, under the "reduction of staples" campaign, those people who knew you best—your fellow workers or classmates—would decide on your proper share. They knew your daily routine, unlike the Street Council, and were able to judge your needs adequately.

Our teacher supervised the meeting to determine each student's ration allotment of staples, but it was the students who suggested quotas and voted for a consensus. When my name came up, a girl suggested that I should receive 30.8 pounds a month. Big Nose said that the amount was too low because I was active and had a long walk to school each day. He suggested 35.2 pounds, which the class later approved. However, when the teacher notified the party secretary, who also was the principal of the school, he thought it was too much and suggested 33 pounds instead. As a result my ration for a month was set at 33 pounds. While we students held discussions on each other's quotas, it was the party secretary who in fact ruled on these decisions, as in all major ones.

In our family I received the largest monthly ration of staples, since Mama and Papa both were allotted only 30.8 pounds under the new system. This discrepancy between the adults and the children in a family was according to Chairman Mao's own dictum that students needed more food because they were still growing. Even though my ration was the largest in our house, I tried not to eat more than one pound per day. Two or three times a month I indulged myself and ate more, generally when I was working on the farms and was very hungry at the end of the long day's work. I was without the coupons to buy food toward the end of those months and had to borrow from friends to tide myself over. Because exercise increased my appetite, I had to cut down on the swimming and ice skating that I loved so much.

Even though my ration was more than Mama's or Papa's, I often dipped into their share at the dinner table. I never seemed to have enough to eat. The actual bulk of food I ate was much larger than past dinners of vegetables, rice and meat. But when dinner was primarily corn-husk muffins, I could eat several pounds at one sitting and still feel empty.

Because rationing was tight, members of a family often fought over portions at the dinner table. When there was so little to eat, an extra bite for one over another was cause for dissatisfaction. No one could afford to invite friends to dinner. It was an unwritten law that guests at a house would leave before mealtime.

My neighbor next door, whom we all affectionately called Big Father, had a great problem because his son and his son's family did stay for dinners. He was an elderly man, his family was his whole life, and he looked forward each Sunday to their visit. But as the food situation deteriorated, he couldn't squeeze out extra portions from his rations for his son, his son's wife and his five grandchildren. He often passed me in the hall and spoke of his dilemma.

He would say, "What am I do? There's just barely enough for the old woman and myself if we budget very carefully. Every time the family comes we can't eat for several days. What am I going to do? How can I tell my own children not to come to see their old grandfather anymore?"

I suggested, "Why don't you just explain your situation to them. Everyone realizes the hard times."

Big Father would reply on the verge of tears. "How can I? I am too embarrassed. I can't even spare a meal for my children? Also, you know my wife is their stepmother. I don't want them to think they are not loved by her."

I wanted to help, and one Sunday waited for the son. I explained the situation to him, but learned that he already knew the facts. The son said that he was forced to come over for dinner on Sundays because he could not feed his large family any other way. Now, however, he said he would no longer stay for dinner.

That evening I heard loud voices in the hallway. Big Father was shouting, "No, no, please stay and eat with us." The son, shoving his family out, was insisting, "No, we simply couldn't. Our dinner is ready for us at home." Finally the mock fighting stopped and the guests left. Big Father spotted me and said, "It was ridiculous, my saying stay when I meant go, and he saying go when he meant stay."

I replied, "That's the way we Chinese are, so polite and so proud. Do you remember the old story of the seven wives who came to dine together? A platter of eight meat dumplings was put before them and each ate one. All saw the lone remaining dumpling and loudly protested that another should have it—each one was completely full and couldn't eat another bite. Amidst their feminine protests, the lights went out and all were in darkness. Suddenly one screamed and the lights returned. One lady had grabbed for the extra dumpling with her hand and was speared by six pairs of chopsticks."

My story cheered his spirits and we both laughed. But the food situation was a serious one, and at my home we also had our quarrels. I shall never forget one after-supper conversation we had in the fall of 1960. I was cleaning up the table, and Papa and Mama were reading the newspapers. Papa was reading an article on Chairman Mao which impressed him and he commented, "Chairman Mao certainly loves the people."

Mama retorted, "He loves the people, all right; that's why we have nothing to eat."

Papa ignored such remarks from her and

looked to me. "Well, we would have more to eat if Sansan didn't eat so much. Every night she eats more than anyone else."

"But I am hungry and I just can't help it."

Mama began to yell, as she always did when she was excited or aggravated. "You are selfish. Why don't you think about me, your own mother? Children don't love their parents anymore. Parents always suffer because of their children. Why don't you think before you eat? You know that I always try to save some of my rations for the chickens. I eat the leftover food from patients at the hospital so as to eat less at the dinner table so I can save something for my chickens. How can they lay eggs if I don't feed them? You eat your share and part of mine every night. Where are the eggs going to come from? Can you lay eggs? I need my eggs. I can't even buy them on the black market anymore."

She got herself very upset with her own yelling, but I could reply only by saying that I was hungry.

Papa also raised his voice. "So you are hungry! That's no excuse. When you are at school, you hand in a two-ounce coupon and you eat only two ounces. Just because you are at home and no one asks for you to turn in coupons doesn't mean you are entitled to eat more than your share. If you lived at school you wouldn't eat more than you were supposed to. At school you would not ask anyone to share his meal with you. Why do you expect it at home?"

When I didn't answer, no one spoke. Yet I

knew the subject was not closed. I went back to the dishes, they to the papers. Later, Papa casually asked me, "Sansan, is the electricity in your room still out of order?"

"Yes. I wear rubber sneakers so I won't get shocks. When do you think the electricians will come to fix it?"

"A long time from now. It's a big job to fix something under the concrete floor. maybe five weeks, maybe five months."

"I have already put in a request but have not heard from the electricians yet. I am scared. What if the electricity gets stronger and sneakers won't help?"

Mama offered, "Why don't you move down to our room?"

"No, I'd rather stay upstairs. There's so little room here, and besides, I need to be alone for studying."

"But you can get hurt—"

"I'll be very careful."

Papa closed the subject. "If you don't want to move into our room, we can't force you."

He was about to continue talking when he hesitated and looked over to Mama, who avoided his eyes nervously and picked up the paper instead. Papa then said, "Sansan, have you ever thought of living at school? Winter is coming and the school is so far away. You have to take an hour's ride on the bus and walk almost another hour. When the snow comes, it will be a real hardship for you every morning."

I was completely dumfounded by his suggestion. Papa continued, "I have always said that community living is a good thing; teaches young people how to get along in society. You can use a lesson or two in getting along with others. Maybe then you won't be so stubborn. Living in the dormitory would broaden your outlook, and it is an experience you should have."

I could only say, "I want to stay home."

"The loose wiring in the floor makes it dangerous to stay in your room. It may be months before it is fixed. You won't move into our room. What other choice do you have but to move to school? Winter's coming and there will be less to eat, and at school you can at least be assured of something every day."

"School food tastes bad. I'd rather eat less at home."

"That's just the point, Sansan; you don't eat less at home. You eat more. You eat more than your mother. You eat more than I do. You can't control yourself, you won't control yourself. At least at school you will learn to eat only what is yours." He took a long breath. "It's better you live at school."

"Mama, what do you want me to do?"

In an unusually small voice she said, "It is your father's house; you do what your father wants you to."

Papa's mind was made up and I wasn't going to beg. I put away the dishes and went upstairs. I walked carefully into the darkened room and sat on my bed thinking. I couldn't blame them about the food. I did eat too much. I certainly didn't want to stay in their room, and it was probably dangerous to stay any longer in mine. It was a long way to school and winter in Tientsin was very harsh. But even though I had to agree with Papa's logic, I was crying.

I was frightened about living at school. Teachers always campaigned for students to live in the dormitory, and on some occasions even put pressure on them. But in spite of the official encouragement, only twenty out of our class of eighty volunteered to live in. What scared me and the others was the fact that the school authorities kept the identification papers of those students who remained at school. If I lived there my papers would be transferred from my home to the school. The authorities then could send the papers anywhere in the country and I would have no choice but to follow them. They could make me teach after graduation in a faraway area; and I would never get home again. I would have to teach anywhere they wanted me to because without the papers I would be a "black person." I could not get coupons or buy food; I could not work. And no one would have enough to support me. Thus, living at school meant giving up any choice in my future teaching assignment.

The next morning, I took my papers to school. My teacher was very happy that I finally had decided to live there.

Chapter Seven

It was a cold and dreary Sunday when I moved from my home to school. My only solace was Skinny Monkey, who had decided to join me in dormitory living to avoid the long trip to school during the harsh winter months and to gain extra time for her studies. We helped each other with our belongings and sat huddled together to keep warm while the bus passed through the familiar winter scenes en route to school.

After a forty-five-minute ride, we still had over a half-hour walk to go. The cold wind lashed at our faces and found its way through our quilted-cotton winter pants and jacket. We were red and stiff from the biting outdoors when we finally reached our assigned dormitory. The room was long and rectangular, and crowded against its four sides were forty double-decker beds. There was no other furniture but a lone desk and chair by the door. We found empty beds and chose two lower bunks that stood side by side. There being no shelves for our clothing, we arranged our belongings as neatly as possible underneath and at the foot of our beds. With eighty girls from different grades in the same room, we were relieved to learn that boarders were allowed to study in empty classrooms at night.

It did not take us long to get settled, and soon we were entertaining some of our classmates who had wandered from the boys' section to seek help with stray buttons and tears in their clothing. While we girls sewed, the boys began to sing familiar songs with great gusto. The wind still howled outside and the single stove burned on uncertainly with almost no coal, but we were warmed by loud choruses of song and each other's company.

When I got ready for bed that night, I was in high spirits. I thought it fun to be there at school with my friends; it was like having many sisters and brothers. But as I folded my bed back, I noticed my blanket was painted all over with dirt and grime from the seats of my visitors. Boys were often careless and did not bother to brush their clothing off after work in the fields.

I was annoyed but fell to sleep quite easily on that cold night. I did not sleep soundly, however, for every time my bunkmate moved overhead, straw from her mattress would filter down over my face and onto my sheets. No matter how many times I kept brushing off the bed, the straw kept falling, and by morning I was exhausted. Skinny Monkey and I quickly switched to top bunks before the rest of the boarders arrived.

We soon became used to the routine of dormitory living. The school bell woke us up at six-thirty each morning, and we would make our beds. Our respective corners cleaned, we brought out our white-enamel washbasin from under the bed and took it downstairs to the boiler room to fetch water. Then back upstairs to wash our faces and clean our teeth. We did most of our bathing when we returned home because the showers at school were seldom operating. When they did, once or twice a month, the girls and boys were assigned different hours on Saturdays. Once, one boy got confused and found himself in the showers at the wrong hour.

Breakfast was served at seven. Since all boarders gave up their identification cards to the school, we did not have to keep our own count of food-ration coupons. At each meal the group captain claimed the proper number of servings from the school's big kitchen and carried the food to his group of approximately twelve students. We ate our food either in classrooms or in our dormitory. At mealtime I usually went to the music room and played the organ. Somehow, the food tasted better when it was accompanied by music.

School food was made of the same raw materials as at home, but it was not cooked as well. Generally we ate our corn-husk muffins with a little boiled vegetable and perhaps a soup of soy sauce and hot water. Though I always seemed to be hungry, I sometimes would not eat my vegetables because I could not overlook the cooked flies floating in the dish. I was among the few who were particular; many students waited to finish my meal for me.

Classes started and ended as before, from eight to four. But after school the boarders had extra duties that students living with their parents did not. Our school had a vegetable garden which we tended. The chores were lighter than actual farming duties in the countryside, but nevertheless, raising cabbages and carrots took many hours of our free time. The heaviest of these duties was watering the field. We would stand in a line from the well to the field and pass our own washbasins filled with water from the first student to the last until the field was properly watered. The basins were heavy and we always got soaked no matter how careful we were.

Other extra duties included sweeping the floors of dormitory rooms or classrooms and working in the kitchen. Every boarder was assigned one day in the week to sweep and clean several rooms, and several days a month to kitchen duty. My first turn in the kitchen was unfortunately during the New Year's holidays, and I had to chop rotten and dried vegetables for the school chickens. Every day for nine days I stood in the kitchen for eight hours, cutting and chopping from morning till night.

The job was tedious and only once did I have an interesting experience. One morning as I stood cutting, a couple of visiting teachers from another province were inspecting the school and peeked through the kitchen door. I overheard one say to the other, "My goodness, this school is excellent. They are already preparing the stuffing for the New Year's dumplings for the students." I laughed and laughed. It had been years since I had tasted a dumpling.

Although we got accustomed to dormitory living, we all looked forward to Sunday. After classes on Saturday the students could leave for home, sometimes before dinner, sometimes after dinner, depending on whether food was available at home. I generally waited until after dinner, and Big Nose and I went home together. Often we missed the last bus and walked the many miles. I enjoyed these walks despite the cold and the wind, because Big Nose was always full of amusing stories and we would march along singing new popular songs that we learned from the radio program *The Song of the Week*.

Throughout the week at school I thought about going home Sunday, and yet, when I actually reached our apartment, I wondered why I had been so eager. Perhaps it was because all my friends wanted to be home with their families. But for me each Saturday night seemed to be the same. Big Nose would leave me by the door about nine, and I would find Mama either already asleep or complaining about something, and Papa reading the newspapers or listening to a ball game on the radio. We would acknowledge each other and ask about each other's health, and then there seemed nothing more to say and I would retreat upstairs to read or to sleep.

On Sunday I always got up early to finish all my chores. Although I lived at school, I still had the same number of chores to do: the family wash, mending clothes, cleaning the floors, chipping coal for the stove, and the rest. I usually finished by late afternoon and generally tried to see a movie or two. There was nothing I enjoyed more than going to the movies; my favorites were two Russian films, *Twelfth Night* and *Othello*. After the movies on Sunday, I returned to school for the week.

When winter had passed, many of my friends returned to live at home, and I began to ask Mama about coming back. The electricity had been fixed and the cold weather had gone, but Mama would only say, "It's your father's house and you must do as he wishes. He wishes you to live at school." I knew there was no use arguing with Papa about coming home when he wanted me at school. It was only after I had lived in the dormitory for six months and it was announced that the school was being moved to another location much closer to my house that I decided to get transferred home despite Papa's wishes.

I told my teacher that my parents wanted me to live with them since the school was now only a short distance away. Then I went and told Papa that since the school was now closer, I had to move back. Only then did he allow me to return to the apartment.

After I had been home only a short while,

Papa started talking about the army for me. I was shocked, for many girls were sent away for as long as three years without home leave, and I didn't understand why he wanted me to join. But for several weeks, each night after supper he talked about the benefits of army life. When I insisted I didn't want to be a nurse's aid or an entertainer for the troops, he would state that serving in the army was an obligation; if I didn't join, who would? He stressed the fact that I was spoiled and should learn to be more independent of the family.

I was bewildered by Papa's talk, but listened obediently each time without being overly concerned. One day after school, however, my teacher asked me to see him and explained that Papa had been to school the day before to volunteer me for army duty. I was stunned and could only say that I was studying to be a teacher and should continue my education before thinking about military life.

As I walked home that afternoon, I became lonely and depressed. Most parents were eager to rescue their sons and daughters from the army, but mine actually went to the authorities and offered me for enlistment. I had heard of only one other parent who wanted his child to join, the father of my classmate Chang. Chang and I had been school friends for many years, and he often caught turtles for me to eat. He was very tall, over six feet, and strong from his hobby of weight-lifting. It was he who often helped me at labor service by carrying my share of construction bricks. Since he was an only son, he was actually exempt from military duty by law, but his father, a progressive party member, volunteered Chang for active duty. Before he left for the army camp, his father said, "Son, you don't have to tell me everything; but you must tell everything to your party leader."

Obviously Chang's father wanted to build his image within the Communist party, but Papa was not a member and did not stand to gain any political credit with a daughter in the military. I just didn't understand why he wanted me to join.

I waited it out a few weeks, and was very thankful when the school did not mention the army to me again. I assumed that they did not wish me to join. However, during the eleventh grade many of my classmates did leave school for faraway camps. Several wanted to go, for the soldiers ate better than anyone else in the country. No one else received meat every day, not even the soldiers' wives and children. Thus some students even memorized the eye charts to pass the examinations. Most, however, pretended to be color blind or unable to read the test correctly, for it was generally known that no passes were given for home visits for the first three years of military life, and many soldiers were asked to "volunteer" service beyond the required three years. Such disadvantages generally outweighed the promise of better rations.

One of the most difficult tasks I had at school was to persuade my friend Wong to go into the army. Wong had too many sisters and brothers, and he realized very early that his parents wanted him to finish school quickly and go to work to contribute money for the family. Thus, when the school authorities approached him about the army, he resisted because it would mean three years without any money. The teacher realized that the only way to get Wong to join would be with the consent of his parents, and so he asked me, a good friend, to see Wong's parents about his enlistment.

I had to go because my teacher had asked me, but I went with a heavy heart. When I arrived at his house, I felt even worse because Wong himself was not at home and I would have to speak about him behind his back. I spoke to his parents about the bright side of army life. "Wong will be well trained and his body will grow strong. The army is like a huge furnace and everyone who enters will come out as strong as steel." I was ashamed to be praising something I myself did not believe in. The parents listened and were persuaded.

At school the next morning, I sought Wong out. "Wong, excuse me, but I went to—" He stopped me from going further. "I know what you are going to say and what is in your heart. I will be leaving soon; let's talk about something else."

He left the following week, and I and many of the class wrote him letters, for he had been very well liked. But Wong didn't reply. It was a year later before I received any word from him. It was a short note:

Dear Sansan:

We have been classmates and friends for six years. This is very unusual, especially because you are a girl. If in a month you have not received a second letter from me, look in the newspapers and you will know why. I have one favor to ask of you; please send me some music scores. Whenever I have a free moment, I like to learn new songs.

Wishing you every happiness,
Wong

I sent the music sheets immediately, and a month later read that his division from the northwest was being transferred to the front lines of Fukien, across from Taiwan.

Like Wong, we students of the eleventh grade started to live our future careers. I began practice-teaching. My first assignment was the sixth-grade class of the elementary school attached to the teachers' school.

On my first day I was very nervous when I walked into the classroom. As I was being introduced by the regular teacher, I stood quietly and looked at my fifty students, a few of them several years older than my own sixteen years. It was a class of farmers' children who had not started school until the government forced education upon them. These students, I could see, had little interest in school; they were needed at home on the farms or out working for a salary.

Standing in front of them, I could feel their eyes walking all over me. When the regular teacher left me alone with them, a boy whispered loud enough for all to hear, "She's no teacher. She's more like my kid sister." They all laughed while I began to explain the lesson. That first day, the students were busy trying to feel me out, to see whether they could ignore me or not. It was not until the end of the school day that real trouble started. Two boys started to fight for some unknown reason, and I tried to stop them while the class took sides and cheered loudly for their favorite. When I got close enough to try to pull them apart, they each hit me in the mouth and continued to settle their own quarrel. Only the ringing of the school bell stopped the fighting, and the students ran out of the room, leaving me alone.

I wasn't hurt by the blows, but I cried. What was I to do against these ruffians? How could I ever control them? They were so much older and bigger than I.

When I walked into the classroom on the second day, I noticed that on the back wall were drawn traditional mourning signs, painted with my name on it. The class had chosen to pronounce me dead. I decided to ignore it all, and began the lesson. Again a fight between two tough boys started, only this time I knew better than to go near them. I stayed behind my desk and said, "Hurry up and finish each other off; I have lots to cover today. Kill each other quickly, please.'' The class stopped fighting and the fighters were so surprised by my words that they returned to their seats. After class that day, I asked these boys to stay after school. When all the students had left the room, I turned my attention to the two boys and began to scold them for their behavior. They stared disdainfully at me and began to unbutton their pants. I was startled, but realized that if I didn't meet this test I would have no control over the class for the rest of the year. So I resolved to stare at their nakedness. They expected me to run out for help or strike them or scream; but all they got was a cold and deliberate stare from me. As soon as they realized I was not going to be unnerved, their faces blushed red and they got dressed. I finished my lecture against fighting in the classroom.

It was apparent that news of this episode had spread to the other members of the class by the next morning, for they behaved much better. I had won control, but they still tried small tricks once in a while. One of their favorites was to line up quickly for the only girls' toilet whenever they saw a teacher approaching. It was often quite embarrassing when I had to wait behind twenty nasty students who knew my problem so well.

Another pastime for these students was to pester the teacher with unrelated, unanswerable questions. Instead of asking about the deeds of a famous personality, they often wanted to know who was his grandmother and what did she do? Instead of asking questions pertinent to the classwork, they delighted in embarrassing the teacher by making up such outlandish questions about minutiae. As the weeks passed, I developed a workable technique against such annoyances. For example, a girl once asked me how to write an obsolete character. I did not know it, but of course I was not going to let her know. Instead I said, ''Young lady, you are in the sixth grade, and you should have learned many years ago how to use the dictionary. If you can't use a dictionary, how did you get into the sixth grade? Since you are so interested in this word, I will help you this time to look it up. Take careful notice and remember how to use the dictionary for the future.''

Because of my sarcastic tongue and quick thinking, my students soon learned to keep their playful tricks to a minimum. But I remember one incident that frustrated me beyond all others. One morning I went to class with a bandage on my forehead where I had cut myself. When I entered through the door of the classroom, a student shouted, ''From Peking to Nanking, I have never seen an egg with a bandage before.'' Everyone hooted and crumpled with raucous laughter. The class was completely disrupted for the rest of the day, and I had to do something to punish the offender. Before I dismissed the class, I announced that he could not go home until I had received a proper apology. Most students feared being kept after school because they were expected home for chores. The other students left and the two of us silently marked time for hours in the deserted room. I vowed that I would not leave until he had apologized, even if I had to remain all night. Finally, his mother arrived, a typical farming wife, coarse and dirty. Before I could explain why I was keeping her son after hours, she began to wail and to complain of the hard life she and her family led, meanwhile puffing on cigarettes. I endured her tears and her chimney smoke for what seemed like hours. She finally decided to stop when she finished her pack of cigarettes. It was no use trying to explain my frustrations to her; she could hardly understand why her son should apologize to me. It was already nine o'clock and time for all to return home; so I dismissed the boy to his mother.

Although I was able to handle my students better than the other practice-teachers from our class, I hated teaching. I had to be on constant guard against my students' pranks and probings. I could not afford a single mistake, for the students could then challenge me by quoting Chairman Mao. No one could answer to a charge based on his edicts; nothing Mao said could be wrong.

On the many occasions when students would throw books across the room or obstruct the doorway, my first instinct was to drag the offenders down the hall to the principal. But I never did, for as soon as I started to put a hand on a boy, he would turn on me with a gleam in his eye. "I know my rights; you can't touch me. If you do, I shall report you to the authorities for violating the Communist Teachers Code. Chairman Mao has brought the revolution into the classroom and we students are protected by this code. Remember the rule that a teacher must never touch his student!"

Any criticisms based on Mao's words were deadly serious. Only on one occasion had someone used it against me. This had happened in a tenth-grade mathematics class when my teacher, Chou, asked me to give an answer to a problem. She had been one of the brightest students in her own school, but she was not very successful as a teacher. She knew algebra and geometry, but could never express herself and thus often accused her students of stupidity. I answered her question correctly, but used obvious and simple mathematical abbreviations in my method. Being a fussy nit-pick, Teacher Chou wanted the long answer, with each step detailed; and so she claimed that she could not understand me. I knew she was being obstinate and demanded to know why she didn't understand my answer. Instead of asking for a more complete explanation of the problem, she casually retorted, "We don't speak the common language."

Immediately the class laughed at me. The teacher had made me lose face and appear foolish before my eighty classmates, but more seriously, she had accused me of a most dangerous political error. Only recently we had studied

Chairman Mao's writings on the common language and learned that a poor man's and a rich man's thoughts could never be the same. The poor man would always worry whether his rice would be raised a cent or two, while the rich man would be concerned about his stocks and bonds. What is important to one means nothing to the other. Therefore, in a capitalist society there is no common language, no common ideas, but a bitter struggle between the classes.

For these reasons I was very angry with the teacher and after class I approached her and demanded an explanation. "Why don't we speak the common language, Teacher Chou? According to Chairman Mao there can be only two cases when people do not speak the common language. The first is if you or I were an animal. But I don't believe you meant to insult yourself or me in this coarse and vulgar manner. The second is if we belong to different classes. Then you must mean that either you or I must be a capitalist. Which one of us, Teacher Chou, is guilty of this most unpardonable crime?" She gave no reply and angrily marched away.

That afternoon in life discussion I confessed the disrespectful manner in which I had spoken to Teacher Chou. But I also justified my anger because she had accused me of a cardinal sin. After the session the political teacher reprimanded Teacher Chou for her indiscretion.

I could not afford to take such accusations lightly, for in matters of correct political thinking and conduct it was crucial for everyone to maintain a good political record. Yet throughout my experience in school, there were two distinct groups of students, each about one-half of the class—those who did extremely well in academic courses and those who did poorly in these subjects and therefore concentrated their efforts on competing for first place in politics. For those interested solely in politics, the goal was to become members of the Communist Youth League. Not I. Membership would have been a nuisance because it meant more meetings and more volunteer work. A Youth League member was obliged to attend all meetings and set examples in personal sacrifices. Although I never dared discuss this with anyone, I would estimate that one-third of the class wanted to join because they were sincerely devoted to Communism, one-third because they were opportunists interested in the small conveniences that came with membership, and the rest, like myself, were lukewarm to politics and participated only to the extent of maintaining a respectable political record.

Thus when my politics teacher asked me why I had not applied for membership, I covered up my true feelings by pleading unworthiness. I told him that I did not think I had reached the stature deserving of consideration for the Youth League. I wanted more time to correct my wrongs and to progress further before applying.

Unlike me, my classmate Huang did everything she could to gain approval for membership. Huang was from the country and, at twenty-eight, was older than most of us. She decided to befriend Tsu, who was the leader of the Youth League in school. He was extremely ugly, barely five feet tall, and had never had a girl friend even though he was almost thirty. He was thus surprised at Huang's attention and delighted in giving her presents and doing her favors. One such favor was to bring her application for the Youth League before the party. While her application was being considered, she was very serious over Tsu; they even journeyed to Peking and had their picture taken together. Although they were not married, in school she called Tsu's mother "our mother" and everyone was astonished at her boldness. However, when the party turned down her application, she completely ignored Tsu and returned to an old boy friend from her neighborhood. The entire school spoke out against her at the next life discussion for using Tsu to further her political standing.

As for romance, it seemed to me that those in high echelons of the party and the intelligentsia could afford love. Because of the political and economic situation, girls seemed to look for husbands on the basis of their social standing rather than their family, personality, age or looks. The farm girls wanted a city man, and the city girls wanted a party member. Also, the severe economic conditions resulted in two extremes of age in marriage. Most people married at a late age; the government preferred late marriage to reduce population, and the majority could hardly afford to be married. A young assistant worker earning seventeen yuan per month could barely support himself. On the other hand, a few young people married at the minimum legal age of eighteen to avoid the problems of bickering over food and clothing with their brothers and sisters. When everything has to be divided evenly among many, suspicions and tensions often drive youngsters away from home.

In many cases, even if two people loved each other they would not marry because of political reasons. In our building lived a member of the Communist party, whom we called Brother Five. He was over thirty and without a wife. All the neighbors worried about him and tried to play matchmaker, but Brother Five still remained single. One day he brought home a beautiful young lady, and everyone was overjoyed and began to speculate on a marriage date. But after a few weeks, he never saw her again. An elderly neighbor could not control herself and bluntly asked him why. He regretfully said that her political background was unsuitable for a wife of a Communist party member.

While I understood why people allowed political considerations to dominate even the most personal aspects of their lives, and I was constantly urged in and out of school to become more "progressive," I did not change my policy of avoiding politics as much as possible. I continued to follow directions and to maintain a good political record, but I hardly lived only for the goals and politics of the state. I seriously doubted that anyone could. At school, in the movies, on the radio, in magazines and newspapers, I heard about those people who were ideal citizens and honored as folk heroes. Every time I learned about their lives I only laughed to myself. Their stories were absurd, too ridiculous for even a baby to believe. Of course, I kept my opinion secret. At political discussions in school, I was dutifully extravagant in my praise and sincere in my wish to follow their examples.

One of the greatest folk heroes was a steelworker whose life was the subject of at least ten separate afternoon political discussions. There was an accident at a factory and the furnace went out of control. In saving three of his fellow workers, he was severely burned, with more than 80 per cent of his body charred. He was immediately rushed to the Shanghai hospital. After examining him, the doctors held a conference and disagreed on his chances for survival. One doctor, who had been trained in America, pronounced the case hopeless because he had learned that anyone with more than 70-per-cent burns could not live. But the representative from the Communist party, who was not a doctor, rejected the physician's diagnosis and demanded the worker's life. "I don't care what the medical books say. It is not in the socialist spirit to allow this man to die. Regardless of percentages, this man must be healed. He is a steelworker and working for the people in a vital industry. He was injured because he cared about China. He must get well.''

The doctors went to work. His fellow workers sent daily pleas for his life, and people everywhere offered to help. When it was learned that he could not eat because his lips and tongue had been severely burned, the restaurants contributed every day many of their most delicious dishes hoping they could make him forget his pain. Still he could not eat. Finally he was given a menu and asked to choose a meal. He selected fish-ball soup. When the soup arrived, he was still not able to swallow and sadly refused it. But then the party secretary spoke up: ''You must eat the soup; the people made it especially for you. The Party wants you to have it, and no one can refuse an offer from the Party.'' When he heard that the people had given it to him, he was able to eat. Thereafter the steelworker ate the people's fish-ball soup at every meal.

Because of his injuries, all his veins were exposed to the air and therefore very painful. When the furniture manufacturers learned of this, they designed a special bed for him. It had an air mattress and could be adjusted to many positions. Other workers designed a unique room for him, with a special ventilating system of distilled air. He never was short of transfusions or transplants, because people lined up for many blocks to offer their blood and flesh. Letters came from all over the country; the people praised him as a great person, one who had helped China industrialize.

Finally, after three months he recovered. But as he was leaving the hospital, he expressed his doubts to the doctor. "I am afraid about my face; it has so many scars." The doctor thought he was worried about his appearance and tried to comfort him by promising to perform plastic surgery. But the steelworker shook his head. "I am not worried about my looks. I was only afraid that the scars might impair my efficiency at the steel factory. With those scars near my eyes, I only hope I can still see into the furnaces."

Another famous folk hero was a woman who worked at a small chemical plant. One day a fire started because someone spilled alcohol, and our heroine immediately stripped off her clothing to beat out the fire. As a result she was seriously burned.

When her husband came to see her at the hospital, her greeting was, "What are you doing here? You have work to do at the factory. I don't want you to miss work on my account. China's industrialization is all-important. Leave immediately, and go back to work." When her parents came to visit, she allayed their fears. "Don't worry, my mother and father. I shall be well because Mao Tse-tung is always with me." While she was on the critical list, she never neglected her political obligation to keep informed. In fact, she died while reading the newspapers.

There were many other folk heroes, but all were as unbelievable and as comic to me. I chuckled each time I read of their feats of personal devotion to a tractor, to a furnace or to Mao Tse-tung. Yet whenever I gave them more serious thought, I would inevitably become depressed. These people and their attitudes personified the characteristics and qualities that would succeed and find happiness in our society. What then would ever become of me?

I did not usually brood about the future. The questions of day-to-day existence generally kept me busy and preoccupied. But sometimes I thought about the prospect of earning thirty-two yuan per month as an elementary-school teacher. With this amount I could survive, but not if I married and had children. While I would continue to teach, I would have to pay twenty-five yuan to the State Nursery each month. With what was left, what kind of life could there be? I supposed I shouldn't get married.

Mama and Papa would then be my only family. We hadn't been a real family for many, many years—not since I was eight or nine. I didn't know what had happened or who was to blame; I only knew that the future would not bring us any closer.

Although I knew Mama's chronic glandular ailment made her cross and sapped her energies, her daily behavior nevertheless offended me. I forgot about her illness and only felt ashamed of her when she screamed all over the house, using vulgar street talk to punctuate sentences, or when she spent practically all her time at home in deep sleep, lying like an immense blob of dough across her bed.

While I couldn't forgive her, I at least knew why she acted this way. But Papa's actions became more and more incomprehensible to me. The first time he had sent me away, I understood the necessity of boarding with Aunt Number Nine near school. But her virtually evicted me when he sent me to live at school in 1960. And after I tricked him into allowing me to return home, he immediately began talking about sending me off to the army. Despite this strained family life, I didn't want to lose what home I had, because I believed nothing could be dearer to me than my home, even though it was an unhappy one.

This then was my future.

It had been a long, long time since I had dreamed of carrying my umbrella and climbing mountains.

Chapter Eight

In the spring of my sixteenth year, I received a letter at school from Grandmother, asking me to call on her as soon as possible. I was very surprised and curious. It had been many years since I paid more than a New Year's Day visit to her. Mama had discouraged me from visiting more often than on the traditional day for paying respect to all relatives. She used to say, "After all, she is not really your grandmother. We call her Grandmother out of deference to her age. She is only the mother of my brother-in-law. You have too much to do around the house to go visiting all the time. It's enough to keep the tradition of New Year's Day."

Mama's feelings found their way back to Grandmother and she no longer expected to see me more than once a year. When I received the letter, I did not tell Mama about it and planned to go secretly to Grandmother on the next Sunday.

Her house was quite far—more than an hour's bus ride and then a walk of almost a mile. When I reached the house, Grandmother's youngest daughter, Goo Ma, answered my knock. She was a handsome woman with large eyes and the disciplined air of the teacher that she was. Goo Ma recognized me and showed me in. "So you did receive the letter I wrote for Mother." She told me that Grandmother had been very ill with pneumonia and, at eighty-three, she thought it wise to see her relatives and settle all her affairs.

I was badly shaken by the news, for I loved the old woman well. She was always kind and loving. Even though I was only a distant relative, she had often teased me about being her favorite child and always remembered my birthdays and holidays with generous presents.

After Goo Ma finished her account of Grandmother's condition, she pointed to a door and said, "Mother's room has been changed. Since Grandfather's death, she doesn't need the big bedroom upstairs anymore; so she has moved into the basement. Go down the stairs and you will find her in bed."

I opened the door and saw a dark flight of stairs. The banister was broken and there was only a coarse rope strung from nails on the wall to hold on to for support. My eyes were not used to the darkness, and as I stepped off the last stair, I almost fell. The floor of the room was slippery with rain water. The basement room was small and lined with trunks. Grandmother was propped up with pillows on her bed, dozing, and I sat on the extra cot to wait until she finished her nap. Even sleeping, Grandmother looked neat, her white hair pulled tightly back to a small circular bun framing her ageless face. She was a tiny woman, not even five feet tall, and looked helpless with her eyes closed.

As I glanced around the room, filled with five old trunks, a table containing cooking utensils, and a bicycle against the stairs, I became terribly depressed. The room was drafty and damp; no wonder Grandmother had pneumonia. I could see her with her small bound feet walking on nights of heavy rainfall—one step, one splash, one step, one splash. Her feet were only three inches long, a remnant of the traditions of the last century. To help herself walk, she wore over her toes a cone-shaped sheath made from cloth stiffened by glue to fill her oversize shoes, and even then had to steady herself by holding on to walls or furniture.

Her sweet wrinkled face and small frame hardly seemed to belong to the hands that rested on the blanket. They were strong, thick and extraordinarily rough. They looked more like the hands of a working man, tough and full of dark spots.

I wondered why Grandmother was living in the basement. Goo Ma was high intelligentsia, the educated elite, who, like high party members, enjoyed excellent salaries and many privileges. Why should Grandmother be allowed to live there when Goo Ma could afford better quarters?

"Who's there?"

I rushed to her side. "It is me, Grandmother,

Sansan. I received your letter and came as soon as I could."

"Sansan, Sansan, I am so glad to see you. I have much to tell you. Things you must know. Ever since I have been sick I have worried about you and wondered about my duty to you. I thought that if I should die before I had a chance to tell you, you might discover the secret from people who would not tell you all the truth. Or you might never know the secret, and then you would never know your real name."

She held my hands in hers, and continued to speak in a little voice.

"Sansan, you are truly my granddaughter. Your father is my second son. Your mother is Mama's elder sister. You are a Chang, not a Soo. Do you understand what I am saying?"

I nodded.

"In nineteen forty-six, when you were only a few months old, your father was sent to America by his employer. He had to go alone and leave the family behind because of tight travel restrictions that existed after the war. But as soon as he arrived in the foreign land, he wanted to have his family join him and worked in every possible way to obtain permission for their passage. He had been separated from the family for long periods by the war with the Japanese and wanted to be with them very much.

"It was the dream of both your father and your mother to be together at long last after the war. But when your father was told to go to New York, there was no immediate hope to bring the family. After six months, he hoped you all could join him in America.

"But in those difficult times after the war, your parents decided that your mother could bring only one child with her. They anticipated a hard time for your mother in a foreign country. She spoke only a little English, she would have no help around the apartment and with the three small children. Besides, ships going to America were overcrowded and often took over a month to cross the ocean. And most importantly, they thought your father's assignment would be for only a year or two and, by the time of his return, the small children would hardly have missed their parents. Therefore they decided to take only the oldest, your sister Bei-yee, who was eight, because they felt she would profit the most from the trip and perhaps learn a second language. Up until the last minute, your mother was going to leave your second sister, Kwei-yee, then barely four, and you, just one, in the care of her sister and her brother-in-law. But Kwei-yee was old enough to talk and understand and she began to cry and fuss about being left behind. Second sister's tears persuaded your mother to make a last-minute decision and take Kwei-yee along too. Your mother's heart wanted to take you along most of all because you were her baby, but she realized that the older children would learn more from a visit to another country. So she left you and a part of her behind, thinking the separation would be for a year or at the most two. She arranged for a

149

nurse to take care of you and for her sister, Mei, whom you have always called 'Mama,' to make a temporary home for you.

"No one at that time, so close to the end of the world war—after seven years of bitter fighting against the Japanese—thought that another war, between the Communists and the Nationalists, would break out. But the fighting did start and soon the situation was deadly serious, and your mother wrote Mei to ask if she and her husband wanted to leave the mainland and bring you to Taiwan. But at the time, Mei thought the change of government not so serious and declined to move. After nineteen forty-nine and the establishment of Mao Tse-tung and the People's Republic, it was impossible for either your parents to return or for you to leave.

"Because of your father's work in the United States, you were adopted by Mei, and for your safety your name was changed from Chang to Soo. Mei couldn't have any children and wanted you to be her own. They decided to keep your real identity a secret."

Grandmother paused and leaned her small face forward. "Sansan, I am old-fashioned. I just couldn't see you living under a stranger's name. I was also afraid that if I did not tell you the truth now, you might later hear an unkind explanation of what actually happened when you were a baby and perhaps it would turn your heart against your true family. Your mother and father are good people and only did what they thought was best. They could not foresee the circumstances that eventually separated you and them. In their letters to me, they always ask about you, and I know that they think of you every day and are heartsick about this fate. They send money and food and clothing to all of us, whenever they can without arousing suspicion. Many of those Hong Kong packages that your house and ours have been receiving have come from them. Sansan, you have never left their hearts. Do you understand what I have told you?"

"Yes, Grandmother."

"I hope your heart will receive this news and your parents. I pray you will not resent them."

"Grandmother, I could not resent them. They are my mother and father. When I was very young, some children used to tease me about being adopted, and in a strange way I guess I have always known this secret. Sometimes when I fight with Mama, she yells, 'Go, get out if you want to; you are not a part of this family anyway!' Now that I know who I am, I want to write to my real mother. Can you give me her address?"

"Call my daughter. She can write English. Tell her I want to see her."

I went upstairs and got Goo Ma, who was correcting some of her students' papers. She came with me to the cellar.

"Daughter, Sansan wants to write to her mother in America. Please address some envelopes for her."

Goo Ma looked at me in surprise and did not speak for a minute.

"Mother, I don't think it is wise. It would only be trouble. Sansan, be satisfied with things the way they are. Your mother doesn't write you; why should you write to her? If she wants letters from you, she has your address. I think you are foolish to think you can achieve anything by writing now."

Grandmother spoke out quickly:

"A daughter has the right to know her own mother. Family is family. I want you to address those envelopes for Sansan. You know her mother never wrote because she thought it would be easier for Sansan and Mei. She was across the seas and didn't want to interfere when she could not do anything about Sansan's future. Now that Sansan understands the situation and wants to establish ties, you cannot refuse her family rights."

"But, Mother, only trouble can come from this. Sansan has no right to bring trouble to us. If she causes suspicion, we can get into trouble with the authorities."

"Daughter, you just write those envelopes; I will take the responsibility for trouble."

Goo Ma had no choice, for her mother had given her a command. I could see that Grandmother was as stubborn as ever. Goo Ma told me she would have the envelopes ready for me when I left, and went upstairs. I thanked Grandmother.

"Sansan, have your mother send her letters

here; then your Mama won't know about it. You have to be careful not to hurt her."

I agreed. We talked some more; mostly Grandmother answered my questions about my real family. She showed me some letters and old photographs, and I was proud that the beautiful and happy faces belonged to my mother and father. I could have listened for days, but it was getting dark and I had to return home. Before I left, Grandmother waved me near her and whispered, "See if anyone's listening by the stairs."

I checked and told her no one was there. Grandmother then dug out a few yuan hidden in a small box from the bottom of an old trunk near her bed.

"Sansan, you will need money for stamps. Here, take this. I don't want my daughter or any of the others to see my hiding places."

"Grandmother, I can't take your money. You need your savings. Thank you, but I can't take it."

Her serene face changed into a mask of mock anger.

"You take this money. I have hidden lots more. Don't argue with your elders; just take it."

I could not refuse; her pride would have been hurt. She stuffed the bills into my pants pockets and patted me. "Now go and get the envelopes. Don't forget to come and see me soon. Maybe next time you will have a letter."

I hugged her and wished her better health

and left. Goo Ma had the envelopes ready and handed them to me without another word as she showed me out the door.

That night, I secretly wrote my first letter to my parents.

MY DEAREST MOTHER AND FATHER,

Today I went to see Grandmother and she told me about our relationship. She let me read your letters and showed me your pictures. It was a wonderful afternoon. I wish that you would write to me directly in the future. I wish that we can correspond regularly because your letters to this house are never shown to me. You should send my letters in care of Grandmother. It is better that Mama and Papa do not know of these letters.

My health lately is quite good. Only a little bloated, but not too fat. I am quite short, but not the shortest in the class. I enclose a picture. I have not taken a picture lately; this one is a year old. I hope you will look upon it often.

I am in my second year of teachers' school, where I've already been practice-teaching as well as attending classes. It is almost vacation time here. We have forty days, but there is also other work to be done outside of school. I don't know yet what it will be.

I think that my sisters should be on vacation soon too. They are probably quite adult and very tall. Please send me a picture of all of you.

Thinking of you and hope to receive a letter soon.

All my love,
YOUR YOUNGEST DAUGHTER, SANSAN

I waited anxiously for a month and then went to see Grandmother. She was looking and feeling much better. Hidden in the seam of her mattress was a letter from Mother for me. I read the letter aloud to Grandmother, who could neither read nor write, and we both cried. I was excited to hear about my real family. My eldest sister had finished graduate studies and my second sister was just starting college. It was a short letter, carefully worded for possible censorship, but filled with warmth and love. My mother was full of questions about my health, education and future. When I finished reading it, Grandmother wanted to hear it again. Our tears were happy ones, yet filled with great longing.

To make us merrier, Grandmother told me how she tricked Goo Ma. She was afraid that Goo Ma would intercept and destroy my letters. She solved the problem by tacking up five nails on the door and asking her friend the postman to put letters on the appropriate nail. Nail number five was me. Grandmother then sat a quiet vigil each day for the mail. With this system, she could keep the letters for me without arousing the curiosity of the postman, and without having to rely on her daughter's honesty and ability to read.

From then on I tried to visit Grandmother at least once a month. During my visits we read letters from my mother and I learned about my parents through the stories Grandmother eagerly passed on to me.

Often I asked Grandmother to retell some of my favorite stories of my parents—their courtship, their marriage and their trials during the war. My father had met Mother during his last year of engineering studies in Shanghai. Before their meeting, Father had been quite aloof to even the most popular girls at college. But when he met my lovely mother, he immediately became very attentive. Mother often pretended to ignore his attentions despite the fact that he was the champion debater of China in both English and Chinese, as well as captain of several college athletic teams. Once Father called after her as she was about to get on a trolley; she pretended not to hear, boarded and found a seat. As the trolley pulled away, Father ran underneath her window for many blocks and earned a laugh.

Soon thereafter they fell in love and planned to be married. However, Father received an opportunity to study in England and they decided to wait until he had finished his studies. They were therefore separated for two years. But each was preparing for their life together, Father mastering his engineering and Mother working to save money for their future.

They were finally married in 1938 on New

Year's Day at a festive celebration with friends and family. Even the sound of Japanese bombs in the distance could not detract from the happy occasion. Just one month after the ceremony, Father had to leave Shanghai for the interior to build power plants. Mother remained behind and only saw him when he was able to sneak across the Japanese lines, disguised as a peddler, to enlist qualified men to leave occupied Shanghai and work for China. For the next three years, Father's work took him farther and farther into the interior, always pursued by the fearsome Japanese bombers. Because the bombers always attacked the power plants, Mother was forced to live in secluded villages many miles away. In those times, Father saw the family only one night a week. He rode two hours on the train and trekked five miles into the mountains on Saturday night, stayed half a day, and returned to the plant by Sunday evening. As a result, he was not with Mother when my sisters were born, but finally was beside her at my birth. In fact, he had to assist my delivery at home because of an air raid.

These stories made me feel a part of a close and loving family. Unlike Mama and Papa, they did not squabble and bicker every night. Unlike Mama and Papa, they were together because of love and not because of convenience.

During these visits I also learned much about Grandmother and her life. In my eyes, she was a great person, a wonderful woman with untutored wisdom and an irrepressible spirit. Her only education had been that of a gentlewoman, received in the home. All her life she lived only for her family—as a girl she was a dutiful daughter; as a woman she was a good wife and mother. Even after Grandfather died and her children became separated by distance or new ways of life, she remained vivacious and cheerful.

I marveled at Grandmother's ability to adjust and to take care of herself. It seemed quite easy for someone to be a gentlewoman and full of graces at a time when the family had many servants and the comforts of traditional mandarin life. But Grandmother never altered her tender ways despite the drastic changes of times. In the often flooded basement, she had no help. She cooked her meals every day on the back-yard stove, and did her washing and all other chores. Tears filled my heart every time I pictured the old woman groping for the stairs and pulling herself up by the rope, so terribly unsteady on her dainty but useless feet, and shuffling to the outhouse in the yard.

Yet Grandmother never allowed herself time to feel forlorn; she was always busy and content. Many years ago she probably had done beautiful embroidery, and at eighty-three she still sewed. She could thread a needle faster than I could; time had taken all of her teeth, but spared her eyes. Only now, instead of decorative silks, she would make an undershirt for me out of discarded old clothing.

Despite the poverty in her old age, Grandmother was most of all a proud person. Everything she owned was in the cellar room, stuffed in the trunks or unseen in the many hiding places she devised. There couldn't have been very much, mostly scraps from a lifetime of compulsive hoarding—strings, paper, an old cup, yarn that was a baby jacket or part of a sweater. For a visiting grandchild she always had a handmade present in an old shoe, a pot within a pot, or in some other peculiar hiding places. Yet she never asked for even the smallest gift from any relative. In all the visits I made, she only asked me for one favor, and this with great reluctance. She needed a used toothpaste tube to make a covering for the spout of her miniature teapot; she was most meticulous and hygienic about all her belongings. After mentioning her need to me, she immediately tried to retract the request, because she knew that empty tubes were valuable: toothpaste cannot be bought unless an empty tube accompanies the industrial coupon and money.

Grandmother's pride was blended with her own brand of reason and logic. During one of my visits, she asked me to compose a letter to my family for her. She had concluded that although she had fully recovered from pneumonia, she had only two years to live. No matter how I tried to dissuade her from thinking this way, she insisted that I write of her plans to my parents. She wanted them to know that she had saved enough money to live out her two years and that any additional funds were unnecessary. Everything had been carefully planned for within this two-year schedule, including money for her burial expenses.

It was typical of Grandmother to think always of her children, even though they might not return her concern. Although she lived in the same house with her married daughter and her two children, they seldom visited the old woman. Goo Ma's only regular call was to garage her bicycle in Grandmother's room. In spite of her old-fashioned upbringing of absolute obedience to elders, Grandmother seldom questioned or interfered with Goo Ma's affairs, not even when her daughter's actions hurt her.

Goo Ma was very ambitious and would have done anything to further her standing. During 1960, when many farmers were running away from the dreary countryside and looking for a better life in the cities, a fifty-year-old woman found refuge in Grandmother's basement. She was given a place to sleep and food to eat. In return, she helped Grandmother with cooking and other chores. It was an excellent arrangement, but it lasted only a week. Goo Ma disregarded her mother's new-found small comforts and seized the opportunity to attain more political recognition by informing the police that her mother was harboring a runaway farm woman. The farm woman was immediately taken away and probably returned to the countryside.

Goo Ma also took advantage of Grandmother. She bought oil from her for only six yuan. Oil is precious and is strictly rationed to two ounces per month per person. Even on the black market, Goo Ma would have had to pay at least twenty-two yuan. Also, as a member of the high intelligentsia, she was entitled to ten times the oil coupons the ordinary citizen receives.

Goo Ma's conduct was in sharp contrast to the generosity of my grandmother and my real parents. I grew to dislike Goo Ma intensely and tried to avoid her on my visits. Only once was I forced to ask her for help.

By winter of 1961 my quilted pants and sweat shirt were three years old and had patches almost everywhere. I wrote Mother and asked her if she could send me some winter clothing. She did immediately. I remember how excited I was as I waited on the long post-office queue to collect my package. I waited for three hours. The post office had so many packages to give out that it often remained open after six and all day on Sunday. I paid nine yuan for the package and ran home to open it.

The package contained several sweaters and two pairs of woolen pants that had been worn by my sisters. Mother thought old clothing had a better chance of being passed through customs than new ones. I couldn't see anything old about them; they were beautiful to me. But as I tried them on, I knew that I could never wear them. They were tapered and unlike any sold anywhere in China. If I wore them, my classmates would taunt me about wearing American clothes; at school we had learned that American teenagers wore such tight pants that they themselves could not peel them off, and needed help to undress themselves. I didn't need help in getting on the pants, but I would be branded as a backward element in the campaign of glorious patches. This campaign honored those who wore patches on their clothing, for they were not frivolous and were concentrating on building China. As a result, students who could afford better clothing did not dare wear them, and many would wear only patched clothing in public. My new pants would surely invite criticism; so I decided to wear them on the inside for warmth and use the same old rags on the outside.

As the winter wore on, I sorely needed another pair of pants. Finally, at Grandmother's suggestion, I went to Goo Ma to ask for an old pair of my father's. Before my parents went to America, they left all their clothing and other belongings with Goo Ma. Grandmother was sure that I could cut down a pair of Father's old pants to fit. I was desperate. I couldn't go out in the streets with my behind shining like an apple.

I swallowed my pride and asked Goo Ma for the favor.

She replied, "What pants?"

"The pants that were left behind in my parents' belongings."

"Oh, those. They were sold long ago. Since your father left, he hasn't sent any money to help keep Grandmother. I had to take the whole responsibility and I needed money; so I sold the trunks many years ago. All the money went to keeping Grandmother.''

I knew it was not true, but there was nothing I could do. I continued to wear my one pair of patched quilted pants for the winter.

Despite these clothing problems and the usual ones of food, my life was different. Nothing in my daily routine at school or at home had changed; and neither Mother nor I dared even to dream of meeting someday. But I had discovered a new world of love and family and happiness. I had found someone to talk to, someone who cared about me. It was different from talking to my good friends because there were many things I could not discuss with them, especially my troubles at home.

Unlike Mama and Papa, who had lost interest in me many years ago, Mother was curious about everything I did and everything I thought, and she worried constantly about my well-being.

In our correspondence, we mostly exchanged news of the family. We were careful not to ask or discuss anything that might cause suspicion. Mother spoke of Father's good health, but never mentioned what work he was doing. Our letters were usually only a page long and dealt mostly with recent activities and health. I loved reading her letters, for she wrote with a classical beauty and her calligraphy was exceptional. From these letters I pictured her as gentle and refined.

In all letters Mother expressed concern about

my future, specifically the fact that I was assigned to be an elementary-school teacher. She never failed to ask about any possible alternatives. When I read of her concern, my hopes for college would be momentarily rekindled, but I knew well that such hopes were impossible. Still, the letters continued to center on my future.

Finally I discussed this topic with Goo Ma, since she was once the representative from Tientsin to the National Teachers' Congress. She only got angry and thought I was ungrateful to shirk my responsibilities to the needs of the state. She told me that her own daughter was assigned to study mining and was also unhappy about leaving home for many years in the mines. Goo Ma refused to intercede for her daughter, but instead fully endorsed the assignment. After hearing this, I knew my situation was hopeless.

Since in my letters I could only hint at my dislike of teaching and at the bureaucratic impossibility of changing one's assignment, Mother was not fully aware of the situation and continued to write of college. She even suggested that I go to the Education Bureau and ask for special consideration as a relative of an overseas Chinese family. She knew that the government was very eager to win the sympathy and dollars of the overseas Chinese. I thought at first this bold gesture might succeed in opening the door for me, for I too knew of the special privileges relatives of overseas Chinese received. They were all able to buy much more food and clothing than ordinary citizens. However, after a month without reply from the Bureau, I knew this approach had failed.

It was on my seventeenth birthday, March 6, that I finally wrote:

DEAREST MOTHER,

Today is my birthday and I hope there will be a letter from you. I am now seventeen. Enclosed is a picture of me. I want to see if you think I look grown-up. (My face is somewhat swollen, but don't worry; within a few days it will be back to normal.) Tonight Mama will take me to a restaurant to celebrate, and, in addition, I will get an extra piece of the chocolate candy you sent to the family. Mama, Papa and I have decided on a rule: every week, each one is allowed two pieces of candy and a glass of powdered milk. With these things you have given us, my life is very full and I am content.

I will graduate very soon. By summer vacation I shall begin to teach. I really wish to change schools, but there's no way. I am now determined to go to night school after I start teaching and make up the subjects for a high-school diploma; and then I shall hope for an opportunity to take the examinations for college. You must know, Mother, that if anything could be done about changing schools, I would do it eagerly.

The last few days I haven't been feeling well; I am running a fever, but the doctors can't find anything wrong. My stomach also ached until I almost cried, but I want you to think of me as an adult now, so I did not.

Mama and Papa have not been getting along lately. Mama's temper is awful. Early each morning she starts with me and then continues with Papa. She never stops. Of course, I know her bad temper is because of her illness; but I also feel that she no longer thinks of me as before. Every week she builds up her anger at me until she yells, "If you don't like home, live at school. Or just die, no one cares. Die, go ahead. Who would care?" Whenever she screams like that at me, my heart is deeply wounded. Papa looks on, afraid to say anything.

You might think that I haven't been a good daughter, that I haven't done my chores or studied hard. But I promise, Mother, this is not so. I take care of everything around the house, including doing the laundry, chopping wood and chipping coals. But still Mama yells. How I wish we could meet. Then I could free my stomach of all the hurts I have swallowed silently in these years. As soon as I can speak to you, I know I shall feel so much better.

Every day I look at your pictures. Since

I was too young to remember your faces, I want to memorize you from the photographs.

Please tell First Sister and Second Sister and Father that I love them very much and think of them always.

Since we are separated by thousands of miles, only through your letters can I know what you are doing and thinking. Therefore, please write to me often.

Your loving third daughter,
SANSAN

The night of my birthday, I dreamed I was with my family. Mother had baked me a cake, just like the one Kwei-yee had on her birthday. The cake had seventeen candles on it, as was the custom in America. Mother, Father and my sisters were dressed as in their last picture and standing by a beautiful pine tree which was decorated with colored lights and angels. They urged me to blow out the candles and to make a wish. I was so happy that I had nothing more to wish for. Then I cut the cake and gave each a piece. Just as I was to taste the delicious cake, I was awakened by my alarm clock. The ugly face said three o'clock; it was time for me to put the food basket on the street.

Chapter Nine

I did not receive a letter from Mother on my birthday or for the next few weeks. I worried and wondered why she did not write. Perhaps the post office lost the letter, or Mother or another member of the family was ill, or Mother was angry with me. I kept writing and asking her to reply. Finally, in late March, I received bad news.

". . . Sansan, recently my health has not been good. The doctors have advised me to have an operation and suggested that I go to a specialist in Japan. I am now in Tokyo at the hospital and will probably be operated on within a week."

Terrified, I cried until I was empty of the smallest sigh. Mama had always been sickly and Mother probably had the same weaknesses. My thoughts ran wild. Fortune had separated us, and now threatened a second tragedy. I prayed to the fates that Mother would be well. Operations are serious and, after all, Mother was close to fifty. I was scared for all of us. My heart beat so hard that I thought it would jump out.

I don't know how I lived through the next two

weeks. I couldn't tell Mama or Papa because I was still writing in secret. I couldn't tell anyone except Grandmother. My thoughts were never away from the picture of Mother deathly sick in a strange country. Somehow I continued to go to school and to do my chores at home. But whenever I was in my room alone, I cried and prayed. During those long nights, I felt like an orphan for the first time. Fear for Mother's life gave me a feeling of being completely alone in the world.

I didn't want to go to sleep because I was haunted by a recurring dream. Mother was on a train. The train started to leave the station before I could get on. The wheels moved faster and faster, and I was frantically chasing after it. I ran for hours and hours, until I was finally left alone without even an image of the train on the horizon.

I lived within this lonely sorrow for two weeks until another letter arrived. Mother told me that her operation was a success. I was somewhat relieved but still not unafraid. The details of her daily routine at the hospital were frightening—blood transfusions, injections, medicine.

Still wrestling with fears, I waited for further news. In late April, I received the third letter from Tokyo. Mother wrote that her health had greatly improved, but that the doctors advised her to rest for another few months. She therefore planned to go to nearby Hong Kong and stay with one of our distant relatives. Mother needed me and wanted me to help her get well.

She hoped that I could ask permission to visit her in Hong Kong during my summer vacation.

I read the letter over and over again to test my eyes. We would finally meet each other. My mother and I. I knew the chances of getting permission would be very slim, but I allowed myself to dwell upon the wonderful vision of seeing Mother at long last. Grandmother was as excited as I was. She and I seemed to cry whenever I received a letter, but this time we were also laughing. I hugged my small grandmother and our hearts danced. We kept repeating, "It would be wonderful, it would be wonderful."

After we managed to still our hearts and smiling faces, Grandmother said, "Child, you realize that once you meet your mother, she will bundle you off to America. She does not write of such dreams because of the censors, and she wants you to apply for permission for a visit. But once you are with her in Hong Kong, she will bring you home to your real family."

I had hoped that was the hidden meaning of the letter. We both decided not to reveal its contents until I had some idea of what the officials would do. It would be unwise to involve the relatives until I was sure that there was a possibility of leaving.

I walked home with plans of how I would nurse Mother back to health. I would bring her tea many times a day, keep her company, read to her, cook for her, rub her back and do everything I had always wanted to do for my real mother. If fate had robbed me of my mother's care, fate now was offering me a chance to watch over her.

The very next day I went to the Safety Bureau to see an official about applying for a pass to Hong Kong. I explained the full situation and brought Mother's three letters from Tokyo for verification. The man listened and said, ''First you have to get an identification card from your school. Get that and then come back to see us.''

I went immediately to see my supervising teacher and repeated my story to him. Though he was also my political teacher and very progressive, he seemed to value human relationships highly, unlike many other party members. I was sure he did not personally approve of my leaving the country, but I knew he would put my request sympathetically to the school principal, who was also the party secretary. He warned me that an answer might take a while because the principal in turn had to get the approval of the Education Bureau.

I had done as much as I could, and now I could only wait. School activities were very demanding, for it was getting closer to final examinations. In addition to studying at every free moment, our class was assigned to planting new trees around the school. It was hard work and gave me a great appetite. On the third day of planting, I felt ill and decided to visit the hospital the next day.

I arose early to go to the hospital so I would not have to wait many hours in line. But even at six I stood on the express line for over an hour before reaching the admitting room, where an attendant took down the necessary data. When he checked my temperature, he said that I was not very ill. I insisted that my temperature had been over 102 when I awoke, and that's why I had got on the express line. The attendant said it was only 100 and waved on the next patient behind me. I had no choice but to start again at the end of the longer line for routine patients. I reached the same admitting room after five hours. This time the second attendant read my temperature at 104 and immediately sent me to the doctor.

The doctor examined me carefully and was alarmed at my condition: my white-corpuscle count had grown from my normal count of 7,000–9,000 to over 27,000. I realized that I must be critically ill when the doctor urged me to stay at the hospital, for admittance was usually very difficult. Although medical care was free for all workers, very few could actually take advantage of hospital care because a patient could only be admitted after receiving the recommendation of a doctor and approval of the head of the hospital. Because of the extremely large number of sick people and crowded conditions, very few workers were actually granted hospital care.

The doctor could not diagnose my specific ailment but wanted me to remain at the hospital. I refused. The basic entrance fee for nonworkers at the hospital was 200 yuan, while the combined salary of Mama and Papa only came to 110 yuan per month. The hospital was a morbid place and reminded me of a jail. All the rooms were packed with deathly ill patients lying on slabs of wood three decks high with hardly room to walk around the rows of beds. I would rather die than stay there. Besides, the doctors probably could not help me, for people in our neighborhood suffered from high fevers that knew no cure. Some even ran fevers for two years.

When I refused to stay, the doctor gave me an official excuse from school for ten days. Later he had to renew it four times because I burned with fever for forty days. Every day spent in bed seemed to be filled with impossible pressures. How did I ever live through the strain of those waiting days? My mind was never at ease. I worried about getting official identification, I worried about being sick, I worried about final examinations. What if I couldn't get the papers? What if I was too sick to go to see the officials? What if I failed my examinations? That would surely spoil any plans for visiting Mother, since the officials would never give a poor student any special considerations.

I had to take care of myself in the midst of these worries. No one was home during the day, and I had to cook and clean as before. But one of my neighbors was always around to carry the stove from upstairs to the yard and back. I could not have managed alone; the stairs were narrow and dark, and the stove weighed over ten pounds. The stairs were always a hazard; I remember Mama's fall many years ago when her flesh was torn so badly that the raw bone showed. She was lucky because at that time there had been chicken soup to help her heal. There was no chicken soup these days.

After the stove was put in the yard, the neighbor would stay to help me start a fire with kindling and coal. It was difficult because the coal was very damp; since the shortage, the government could only meet its promise of 165 pounds per month for a family of three by adding to the weight by packing the coals in mud and then not allowing them to dry properly. When the stove was finally lighted, I cooked my usual meal of flour and hot water. Sometimes, when Mother sent us sugar, I could sweeten the chalk-tasting gruel. Otherwise I ate this concoction three times a day, for corn-husk muffins were too rough to digest and probably would have bloated my stomach until it sat on my lap, as it had in the past when I suffered from weeks of constipation. Throughout my illness, my diet remained the same except for the few days I enjoyed some wheat Skinny Monkey gave me. Her father in Hong Kong sent her foreign exchange and with it she bought this gift for me.

One night in June, toward the end of my illness, when I had already gone back to my classes, we had just finished supper and I was about to return to my room when Mama said that she wanted to talk with me. Papa immediately excused himself and announced that he was going to the public baths. When the door closed behind him, Mama took a letter nervously from her pocket and turned to me.

"Sansan, I have received a letter from my elder sister. She has told me about your letters to her and her letters to you. Your Papa and I have talked this over and decided that I should speak to you."

I looked directly at her as she continued.

"When my sister was leaving for the United States, she asked me to take care of you. To tell you the truth, Sansan, I didn't want to. After all, raising a child is not easy. But she was my own sister and I could not refuse. After you came to live with us, Papa and I both grew to love you very much and wanted you to be our own child. After all, my sister left you when you were only one year old. We were willing to give you a good home and accept you as our own daughter.

"So when the revolution started and my sister did not come back to get you, we changed your name and have raised you as ours."

Her voice was unsteady as she spoke, and I knew she was about to cry.

"We've given you everything we could for seventeen years, and now you want to leave us. You want to go to someone you don't remember, someone who doesn't remember you, someone who left you behind when your sisters were taken along."

Her tears now turned to sobs; I hated to see her that way.

"Sansan, we raised you and now you want to desert us. I never thought you were that kind of a person. Didn't we love you and care for you? Didn't we share with you everything we had? What else could you ask of a mother and a father?

"I know that I have a bad temper, but you know, dear, it is because I am not well. I haven't been well for many, many years. Whenever I yell at you I realize I am wrong and I promise myself I will stop, but I can't. My illness makes me do things I don't mean to. I have tried to be a good mother.

"Sansan, you can't leave us. We are not young. Papa is almost sixty-five and I am in my late forties. We need you. You needed us when you were small, and we cared for you. Now we are getting old, and we need you. When we adopted you, we thought we could count on you, that you would care for us in our old age. I never dreamed that you would desert us.

"If you leave, you will go to strangers and leave your real family. Don't go, Sansan, I beg of you. Give this plan up. Don't go."

Mama was hysterical and her tears had soaked her dress. I didn't move or say anything but waited until she finished crying. Her wailing was pitiful, like that of a desperate widow, but my heart was not moved. I only thought that she did not want me to go because she wanted me to be her insurance for her old age. Finally, when she calmed down, I said:

"Mama, I will always do my duty to take care of you. You have my promise. I shall always be your daughter, but if I remain in Tientsin I have no future. As an elementary-school teacher I would receive thirty-two yuan a month—not enough to feed myself, much less any family. If I can get to Hong Kong, perhaps I shall have a chance to go to college. Nothing between us is changed if I go; every child has to leave home sometime.''

Mama didn't understand, and only started to wail again.

''Sansan, we raised you and you belong to us. You belong to us.''

I knew that no matter what I would say, she would not understand. For her I was and always would be someone who belonged to her or to someone else. She would never understand that I belonged to myself.

''I have to go upstairs now. Tomorrow I have a history test.''

I left her crying in the room.

Mama and Papa did not raise the subject again. I tried to go on as if we had never talked.

During these days in late June, when I was already burdened with many personal problems, the political teacher announced a series of five compulsory lectures after school. At the first meeting we were sworn to strict secrecy: no mention of the lectures outside the school grounds and no notes to be taken during the meeting. These unprecedented precautions meant we students were about to hear of new political events or policies that had not yet been approved for release to the general public.

The essence of these lectures was to criticize

Khrushchev and to prepare the way for a new attitude toward Russia.

Khrushchev had been too harsh in renouncing Stalin, who was the greatest leader of Russia and who took up the flag of Marxism from Lenin's hands. China does not deny that in later years Stalin committed a few serious mistakes and that these mistakes to some degree held the progress of socialism in abeyance. However, Khrushchev was wrong to allow these mistakes to eclipse the great work that dominated most of Stalin's life.

Stalin's main mistakes were "big national chauvinism" and bureaucracy. Stalin was so proud of his country and himself that he did not appreciate the small countries, nor even China. His immense pride buoyed him into believing that he alone was wise; and he killed some men who were guilty of minor errors and some innocent people for what he believed was for the good of the Russian people. This arrogance and inclemency led to timidity among the cadres, who became afraid to report any unpleasant truths. As a result of sitting at his desk and listening to rosy-colored opinions from subordinates, Stalin was not always aware of the true situation in his country.

Though Stalin was guilty of these mistakes, there would not be a Russia today if Stalin had not ended World War II and saved his people from starvation. There would not be a free eastern Europe today if Stalin had not marched into Berlin. There would not be Marxism today if

Stalin had not defeated Trotsky, the greatest enemy of Marx. There would not be sputniks and the space age if Stalin had not been the father of rockets.

Stalin's errors in judgment were human. Everyone has faults; only a newborn baby or a dead man cannot make mistakes.

So Khrushchev was unfair when he spoke out so severely against Stalin, and should not have burned his body. The Russian people still loved him, for even as Khrushchev ordered Stalin's cremation, twenty thousand people gathered in Red Square and wept. Khrushchev was forced to order armed police and the army to drive the mourners away. The loyal people then took Stalin's picture and paraded to his birthplace and chanted "Stalin is our greatest leader and he will live in our hearts forever."

Khrushchev should not have demoted Stalin's son from a colonel to a private, or caused Gagarin to lose favor because he was originally appointed by Stalin. Khrushchev says there was no freedom in Stalin's period; there is in fact none in Khrushchev's, for he has punished those who still love Stalin. Khrushchev now is afraid of his people because he realizes that they do not agree with him, and therefore he bribes men with money and the promise of a good life. The Russian people soon will see through his deceit.

Khrushchev has accused Stalin of raising the cult of personality, but he himself is guilty of the same offense. In a new Russian book, *The March to Berlin*, Stalin, the great general, is only mentioned forty-nine times and Voroshilov, Stalin's assistant, who helped train the army of one hundred thousand soldiers, is mentioned only two times, while Khrushchev, then a small party secretary of a small city, is mentioned seven times. Khrushchev has ordered the removal of Stalin's pictures from the walls, but replaces them with his own. Khrushchev has also dictated that towns and streets named after Stalin be renamed for himself. This is a sharp contrast to our own leader, Chairman Mao, who refused the request of the people to name a new city after him three years ago. Also, Chairman Mao has never had a big birthday party. From this one can see the greatness of our leader. It is our own Chairman who has taken the flag of Marxism from Stalin's hand, while Khrushchev is changing the truths of Marxism.

Thus the fight between Russia and Albania is but the argument between Marxism and Revisionism. What Khrushchev has failed to realize is that this argument is between socialistic nations, countries who are comrades. Such an argument should be discussed calmly at the conference table and solved, because there is no question between two socialist countries that cannot be settled in a discussion between all comrade nations.

Khrushchev has refused to deal justly with this problem. Instead he has stopped all aid to Albania and refused her a seat at the Twenty-second International Communist Party Congress. In holding back technical and financial aid to a smaller country, Khrushchev is also guilty of "big national chauvinism." While the Twenty-second International Congress was held in Moscow, it was nevertheless a world meeting, not a Russian meeting. Thus Khrushchev had no right to keep a socialist country like Albania from taking its seat, and he does not have the power to oust her from the socialist class. Such an action can only be taken with the approval of every other socialist country.

Actually Khrushchev stopped supplies to Albania because he wanted to "kill the chicken to warn the monkey." The chicken is Albania and the monkey is China, and he wished to warn China against a quarrel with him. But China has no fight with the Russian people, only with its premier.

When Khrushchev stopped Russian aid to Albania, Hoxha said to his people: "Even if we have to eat the roots of grass to live, we won't take anything from Russia." China is not guilty of chauvinism and immediately sent food to our brother country.

Other Communist countries also disagree with Khrushchev's policies, but they are afraid to speak out or to act because they fear he will also stop sending aid to them.

How will this problem be solved? It can be settled by three means. One, that there will be a war between Russia and Albania. Two, that Khrushchev will be punished by the Russian people. Three, that Khrushchev will realize his mistakes and correct them.

These lectures stirred unprecedented interest in current events among the students. While we were required to know all the important news of the day for politics class, we seldom read newspapers. We relied entirely on the student with legible printing who was assigned daily to copy news articles onto the blackboard for the class. If we did look at newspapers, it was to check on the shows at local theaters. But because of these lectures, students became immensely curious about the possible turn of events and sought eagerly any new developments from the papers. Some even lined up at five in the morning to buy a three-cent copy of the *Communist Party News*. Most readers received home deliveries of this paper, and only seven copies were sold at newsstands to the general public.

During the following weeks, the newspapers ran many articles on Khrushchev and Sino-Soviet relations, asserting the independence of China from her Communist neighbor. To disprove the belief that there was a Russian in every Chinese back pocket, these articles described the strained relationship between the two countries. For example, China, despite popular belief abroad, paid for all that Russia gave her. The only outright Soviet gift was some machinery sent in the early fifties, with parts that did not fit. Russia made many trade deals which were at Chinese expense. When Russia offered to buy Chinese pork at a very handsome price, the generous arrangement was given consider-able publicity and China was very pleased to send its very highest-grade pork. When the shipment arrived, Soviet inspectors searched diligently for pork bristles and found one. Using this as evidence of inferior quality, they refused the entire shipment. However, knowing the large transportation expense back across their country to China, the Russians were eager to demonstrate their neighborliness, and they gra-ciously bought the "substandard" pork—at a much reduced rate.

The relations between the neighbors were further strained by Khrushchev's readiness to boast. When Chou En-lai was attending the Twenty-second International Congress in Mos-cow, the Russian leader took him on an inspec-tion tour of agricultural facilities. At one farm the fat Russian pigs were eating their supper. Khrushchev took this opportunity to point out casually that the pigs were eating the best-grade rice imported from China. Object lesson: Rus-sian pigs eat better than Chinese people.

With these stories paving the way, the news-papers began calling Khrushchev every epithet in the Marx-Lenin-Stalin vocabulary: deviation-ist, chauvinist, opportunist, rightist and so on. The Russian leader was to be distrusted and dis-liked as much as the western leaders. Pictures of Khrushchev smiling and shaking hands with President Eisenhower of America at Camp David appeared often to represent the sinister friendship between the two.

As a result of these stories and the political lectures, the atmosphere around school was charged with curiosity and excitement. Never before had the students seemed so genuinely interested in international political developments. Although the additional lectures took up my precious free hours, my thoughts were never away from my personal problems of making up studies and waiting for further news about the possibility of getting permission to go to Hong Kong.

One night in early July, I arrived home late from school because of extra duties in the planting program. It was after six when I opened the door to the apartment. I was completely surprised by what I saw. Mama and Papa were sitting in the room with all of the Chang relatives except Grandmother. Mama spoke. "Sansan, aren't you going to greet your uncle and aunts?" I walked over to Goo Ma first; then to my father's older sister, whom I hadn't seen since New Year's Day at Grandmother's; finally, to Father's younger brother. I recognized him from pictures; he resembled my father a great deal, but was slightly taller. He was an engineer, and had an excellent job with a salary of 200 yuan per month. His home was many provinces away from Tientsin, and I recalled meeting him only when I was very young.

We exchanged polite greetings and I asked about their respective families. Then, after I sat down in the chair obviously left for me, there was a strained silence. I looked with questions in my eyes at all faces, but only Goo Ma returned my stare without turning to examine the floor or her hands. Young uncle found his chair very uncomfortable and shifted his weight many times. Everyone seemed to listen attentively to each creaking of his wooden chair. Papa cleared his throat and tapped his foot nervously.

Finally Mama spoke. "Sansan, Papa and I have discussed your plans to meet my sister in Hong Kong. You know that we love you dearly and want you to remain in Tientsin with us. But we are not selfish people. We want to do what is right and proper under the circumstances. Papa and I are probably too close to you to give you fair advice, for our hearts are tied to yours. So we wish to consult others for their good opinion. And the people who could give you unprejudiced advice are the relatives of my elder sister. That is why I have asked the brother and sisters of my sister's husband here tonight. These people are not members of my family, but of the family you wish to join. You should heed their advice and obey their suggestions."

Mama had finished her introductory speech and all rushed in with, "Sansan, listen—" but Goo Ma's voice rose above the others to command attention.

"My dear little niece, Sansan. Your father is my elder brother, and when he was in China, we were the closest among all the children. We were not only brother and sister, but good friends and companions. But that is past. He is a capitalist and we are socialists. He chose to live in the country of warmongers, and we remain true Chinese, living each day to help our people and to build a great China. We work to make China great, and he works to defeat his own people. Although he is my brother because my mother gave birth to both of us, he is not my comrade. He is an enemy of socialism, and therefore must be your enemy. Don't be a romantic fool and think fairy tales about a reunion with your real father. It's all nonsense. What is important is your country. No blood or bone can have any meaning when two people have different political philosophies.''

I gave them no reply. I didn't want to argue with them. I knew Goo Ma for the opportunist that she was. I knew that if capitalists controlled China, she would then be their avid supporter. She changed her face and heart for every occasion.

Surrounded by the circle of my elders, I vowed to hold my tongue. Uncle spoke next:

''I want to tell you the truth, Sansan. America is corrupt. I can see that clearly in the photographs of your sisters. I am ashamed to look at them. You know what I mean. Do they look like students? Do they? Have you seen any Chinese students who look and dress as they do? Your sisters are shameful, their hair all curly, their face all made up for the stage. They say they are students, but they look like something else altogether.''

I bit my tongue. I didn't want to give him the satisfaction of seeing my tears. It's none of your business, Uncle, I said to myself. It's not up to you to say whether my sisters are good or bad. You talk about my sisters, but what kind of uncle are you? The first time you come to see me in ten years and you only insult me. I swallowed my thoughts and tasted blood from my lips.

Mama agreed with Uncle. "My sister always worried about clothes and how she looked. When I lived with her, she made me wear high heels and nylon stockings. She was obsessed with luxuries and spent hours each day to look high-class. I have other things to think about. I have an important job at the hospital. I occupy my thoughts with hard work, not silly ideas about outside appearances."

I wanted to say, "It's true, you never care about appearances. You won't even wear a bra." But I didn't utter a word. I sat still and wondered when the session would end.

They continued. They did not sound or act like a family. They surrounded me and mouthed political lessons and slogans or attacked the reputation of my mother and father. I don't want to remember that ugly night. Although I didn't say a word, they all kept on speaking and their voices grew more and more angry. All were against my going to Hong Kong, and their reasoning about political differences and my family's corruption was repeated over and over again without their saying anything new.

They lectured to me for over three hours and I was exhausted from silence. Finally I could not hold it in any longer, and spoke. My voice surprised them and they fell silent.

"You can criticize me all you wish, but please don't talk about my mother and father in such a way to me. It accomplishes nothing. Why don't you do what Chairman Mao says is the correct Communist method for criticism. Why don't you write directly to them in America and question and criticize them openly. Then you would be truly following the rules."

Goo Ma spoke for the group. "It's nine-thirty, time for us to go."

After they left, I returned to my room, even more determined to get a pass. I wanted a real family more than ever—one of heart rather than slogans.

Again at home we pretended nothing had happened. We continued in our daily routine, and no one mentioned the family discussion meeting, except Uncle. After returning to his home, he sent three postcards. The first said: "Have you thought everything through?" The second: "Don't forget Bandit Chiang Kai-shek fought to stop the People's Revolution." The third: "America and capitalists are corrupt warmongers." I read his words and wondered if the postcards were written for my eyes or for the authorities.

I paid no attention to his words, for I was not interested in politics. I merely wanted to be with my real mother, who was sick and needed me. I had studied the political theories of Marx and Lenin for over six years and was one of the few people in my class who had consistently received ninety-eight in political classes. I knew well the theories offered by the Communists as well as by Youth League members. In fact, it was I who often had to explain to members the complex differences between rightists and leftists at various periods of political campaigns. I knew from my experience that politics could be explained in many ways, depending on whose side was being accepted as correct.

To me politics was very much like an old Chinese story I knew. A mother was always complaining about her daughter-in-law to neighbors. One day she said, "The fates have rewarded me with a terrible daughter-in-law. Do you know that every time she visits me, she steals my matches and cigarettes to bring to her home? Fortunately, I have a wonderful daughter who brings me cigarettes and matches from her husband's family's home."

From my own daily experiences I knew that the Communist party in China was not succeeding as it had hoped. But I did not know what other countries were like and therefore did not think about the political questions that so worried my relatives. I only wanted to join my family. Whether they were capitalists or socialists or fascists had no meaning for me; only that they were my mother, my father and my sisters.

My mind was made up to rejoin my family and I thought nothing could ever change my decision. My stubborn nature was recognized by all who knew me, and Mama and Papa knew it was useless to discuss the matter further. Besides, they thought that my application for a pass could only be refused and decided to wait for the officials to destroy my plans. Meanwhile, I studied hard for the final examinations and visited the Overseas Bureau daily. It was mid-July when I received a letter from Goo Ma asking me to call on her. I could not refuse and made preparations to visit the next Sunday.

When I arrived this time, Goo Ma showed me to the basement and said that she and Grandmother had something to discuss with me. After I greeted Grandmother, she did not continue the conversation but waited with worried looks for her daughter to speak. I was puzzled. Goo Ma, looking particularly severe, began:

"Sansan, your grandmother and I have been thinking about your plans to go to Hong Kong for many days. I know that our last conversation at your house did not move you at all, and you are still planning to apply for a pass. You had better listen to us today before you go ahead with your plans.

"You did not believe us when we discussed with you the importance of correct political thinking and background. You did not think it important that you are a socialist and your father is not. Perhaps politics does not matter to you, but it matters to the American government. The American police would arrest your family and you if you should join them in the United States. You are not an asset to your father. You can only do him great harm by leaving your country, an enemy of America, and moving in with your family. If you don't care about politics and your duty to China, you cannot ignore what the Americans will do to your family if they know you are a socialist from the People's Republic of China.''

I was stunned and didn't know what to say. This possibility had never occurred to me. What did I know of the outside world? My whole life had been spent within a circle of twenty-five miles. How could I evaluate the conclusions Goo Ma had reached? Would the Americans really jail my family on account of me? Many people in Tientsin had been arrested for having families with suspicious political backgrounds.

Grandmother beckoned me to her side and, with her frail arms around me, spoke. ''Child, I thought at first that nothing would be more right and good than for you to join your family and live under your true family name. I would have done anything to help you to go to Hong Kong. But my daughter warns me of the consequences to my son, and I am afraid. I love my son more than my life, and if your presence would harm him, I can only beg you not to go.''

''Grandmother, of course I will not go if my family will be endangered. But I don't know anything about America except for history classes at school and the newspapers. How can I know what the government would do?''

''Sansan, I am an ignorant old woman who will soon return to her 'old home—' ''

''Grandmother, please don't talk about leaving—''

''Listen . . . listen. I am old and know nothing of other lands. I want only happiness for my children. If there's even the smallest chance that you may bring trouble into my son's life, please don't go. Please . . .''

Grandmother's plea moved me to promise that I would give up my plans of applying for a pass to Hong Kong. I would have been able to live with the disapproval of Mama, Papa, Goo Ma and everyone else, except Grandmother. To be with my mother, I would have been willing to risk everything, except my family's safety. Before that afternoon, I had nothing to lose and a future to gain if I succeeded in getting to Hong Kong. No one could have made me give up my dream of a reunion with my mother. But now I gave up the dream unhesitatingly.

I did not stay any longer, since I had to return home to study. As I left, Goo Ma put on an approving smile and placed her hand on my shoulder. ''Sansan, you have made a very wise decision. I can see that you are quite grown-up now.''

When I reached home, I knew that I had to write Mother and tell her, but I didn't. Even though I knew I could not go to Hong Kong, I was unable to write the words that would absolutely end my dream. I waited and waited, hoping something would happen, hoping something would alter the promise I made Grandmother.

I was busy with school and studies. I had to do well on the examinations, or risk being sent to an undesirable post to teach. If I had to teach,

I wanted to do it in Tientsin, where at least I would be near home and my friends. The week passed quickly as I concentrated on studies. On Sunday, I went to see Grandmother despite all my work, vaguely hoping something would happen.

Grandmother was sewing when I came down the stairs. She greeted me and asked me to check the stairs for eavesdroppers, and when assured that we were alone, she went into her mattress and came up with a letter for me to read. I didn't recognize the handwriting on the letter to Grandmother; as I glanced at the first few lines, I realized it was written by my father. My mother used her maiden name and always wrote for the entire family, because it might have been politically unwise for Father to write. I was therefore most excited to hear from him.

I read the letter aloud to Grandmother. It was a short note asking Grandmother to help me in making plans to go to Hong Kong. My father stressed his wish for me to meet Mother.

After I finished reading, Grandmother thought in silence as I reread the letter to myself. When Grandmother had obviously made up her mind, she said, ''Sansan, your father wants you to go to Hong Kong and to Hong Kong you will go. I trust your father and his decisions. There need be no more said; you shall go to Hong Kong.

''I have money for any needs you might have. Go home now, study hard—your father wants you to arrive with your diploma in hand—and wait for an answer from your school. Don't tell

Goo Ma anything as you leave; leave her to me.''

She hugged me and bade me good-bye. I walked home feeling that nothing could go wrong now. Grandmother was firmly behind me and that's all I needed.

Meanwhile, final examinations were in process at school. Because of my long illness and absence from school, I was given permission to take a make-up examination at a later date, but I was still scheduled for the oral-criticism period before my classmates. I was relieved to be given some extra time to prepare for the written exams and did not worry about the criticism period. Although the report was crucial to a student's future, I knew I had done a good job with the elementary-school children, and trusted in the fair judgment of my classmate friends, who were on the same teaching team as I.

I was not nervous that day, but I could sense the tension in others. The remarks offered by the students would be recorded in each student's personal file, and this file followed the individual for the rest of his life. If bad remarks were written down, the student often would suffer from them for his entire future.

The ten of us in the teaching team for Elementary School Number Two met on time in the classroom and the cadre leader asked for opening comments. Big Nose raised his hand. Many were surprised, because he seldom spoke until he had to. But this morning he seemed to be fully aware of what he was doing and deliberately got up to speak.

"My classmates, I feel it is my duty this morning to bring to the attention of Soo Chin-yee my observations of her teaching abilities."

I smiled to myself and blushed, because I knew my old friend would give me too much praise. He did not look at me but continued to speak.

"I wish to raise six items for her. One, Chin-yee stays in her classroom too much and does not go out to play with her children. If she really loved her students, she would spend not only classroom time with them but also hours on the playing field. The state needs teachers who enjoy teaching. Otherwise China cannot succeed in its educational programs.

"Two, Chin-yee is a most stubborn person and seldom listens to advice. A person who cannot learn from constructive criticism is a backward element in society.

"Three, Chin-yee will not take naps at noontime. Instead she annoys those who wish to sleep.

"Four, Chin-yee does not discuss her problems with others. She keeps too much to herself. She never volunteers her inner thoughts.

"Five, although she does well in the classroom and her students learn from her, she has never willingly shared her talents or experiences with others. She never goes out of her way to help the other practice-teachers.

"Six, whenever the closing bell rings, Chin-yee is already packed and ready to leave school.

"That's all I wish to say."

Everyone was as surprised as I was. It all seemed unreal; my eyes were fascinated by the student secretary, who was recording the comments into her notebook. I stared at the girl writing until she finally stopped and joined the others in looking at me.

Another student sitting by me was obviously angered by Big Nose, and poked me to stand up and raise criticisms against him. I did not move. Everyone waited for me to speak up against him, and finally Big Nose himself asked, "Well, Chin-yee, don't you have anything to say to me?"

I never thought he would raise any items against me. He had been my close friend for six years. These items would affect the recommendations and remarks of my political teacher and my permanent personal file. His words would poison my record for a lifetime. He knew all this and yet he did it. No one else said anything; they all knew how close we were.

Another student said, "Speak up, Sansan, speak up. We want to hear your side. Defend yourself."

Obediently I stood up and without emotion replied, "I have no criticism of classmate Tsiang."

All were stunned and the formal session turned into whispered confusion. Finally Big Nose took the floor and spoke righteously as if he were the injured party. "Perhaps what I have

196

long feared is true: that Chin-yee does not care about me. Her refusal to speak and give me constructive advice is evidence that she is not concerned about my growth.''

I don't remember what happened during the remainder of the class. I could only think of my betrayal. In my wildest suspicions, I never would have believed it would be Big Nose who would turn against me—not him, not my adopted brother. As soon as the session ended, I ran for the school yard and hid behind a bush and cried. I was not grieving for the loss of a friendship, but for the loss of my self-image. I had prided myself on my keen judgment and sharp eyes; I had thought I could see to the heart of any person, even a total stranger. Now I realized that I did not even see to the heart of Big Nose, a close companion for six years. I really didn't know anything at all about life. I was as naïve and defenseless as I had been the day I wanted to write a letter to the Education Bureau protesting the campaign to combine education and labor. All the skills I thought I had acquired to guard myself against political criticism were proved false. If I had had any sense at all, I would have foreseen Big Nose's action that day. But I was a stupid child.

My thoughts were interrupted by Big Nose, who found me behind the bush. He sat down on the ground beside me and gently said, ''Maybe I was wrong in my analysis of your teaching performance. But if I was wrong, why didn't you speak up to defend yourself or to criticize me?''

How could he have spoken to me that way. If he had merely said that he was sorry, but felt he had to criticize me because of the system, then I would have understood and forgiven him.

"Big Nose, I didn't want to waste my time. Every minute of my life is very important to me."

Angered, he stood up, bowed in mock reverence to me and walked away. Since that day, I have tried to find the motive for Big Nose's actions and only one makes any sense: he must have turned "progressive." Although he was a political laggard in the six years I knew him, he must suddenly have realized the necessity of an enthusiastic response to the political system as graduation drew near. He then sought the best opportunity to show his new attitude by turning against me, his closest friend. This could be the only answer, because in our entire relationship only once did Big Nose show concern about political appearances. That was the time he advised me not to use the glossy pages from ancient American *Life* magazines to cover my schoolbooks.

A few days after the criticism period, I received word from the political teacher that the school approved my request to go to Hong Kong and would issue me an identification card. The political teacher also said that he thought Big Nose's criticisms were too severe and that he did not believe the six items. At that moment I didn't care about Big Nose. I was on my way— on my way to Hong Kong, Mother and home.

With the card clutched in my hand, I rushed immediately after classes to the Safety Bureau and repeated my request for a visitor's pass on the basis of my mother's three letters. The official listened to the story and then asked, "Why not have your mother return to China and stay with you in Tientsin?"

I stifled a laugh. How would I ever feed her? There was hardly enough food for me at home. But I replied, "She is very ill and cannot travel. That is why I must go to Hong Kong as soon as possible to nurse her. She needs me very badly, and you must help me."

The official took down some notes and asked me to check back in a few weeks. He did not encourage me or discourage me, but acted like a bureaucrat.

In the meantime, I had received a short note and an enclosed newspaper clipping from Mother. The note said that the clipping would be proof to the Tientsin authorities that I would be allowed into Hong Kong if I was successful in getting a passport from China. The clipping was an announcement by the Governor of Hong Kong granting permission to Chinese mainland students to visit their families in Hong Kong during the summer vacations. The Hong Kong border authorities would allow students into the city during the period from July 5 to August 31. I read and reread the article carefully, then I turned it to examine the back. If the printed words on the other side were in any way anti-Communist, the proclamation by the Governor would be useless to me. I could never take the chance of carrying any unfriendly newspaper article from Hong Kong into the Safety Bureau. I wondered if my mother had given any thought to this possibility; it was quite natural for me to be cautious. Fortunately, the back contained only an advertisement.

After two weeks had elapsed, I returned to the Safety Bureau. The official said that he had not received official notice yet, but that he thought he saw my name on the list of approved petitions. I was confident he was right and floated home on daydreams about my traveling plans.

Perhaps it was due to these grand expectations, but when I took the final make-up examinations in early August, I did better than I had ever done before in school. With these high scores, I went to confirm once more to the authorities my intentions of returning from Hong Kong to my future as an elementary-school teacher. And at this visit, over three months since I first had gone to see the official at the Safety Bureau, I was given the pass. It was only a piece of light-blue paper folded in two on which was written: ''SOO CHIN-YEE, THIRD-YEAR STUDENT, TEACHERS' SCHOOL, SEVENTEEN YEARS OLD, THIRTY-DAY VISITOR'S PASS TO HONG KONG,'' with the Safety Bureau stamp. But this simple piece of paper was my ticket home.

After dinner that night, I told the news quietly and as unemotionally as possible to Mama and Papa. I didn't want to gloat. They did not seem surprised; I guess they had given up. Mama offered to give me the sixty yuan for the train fare, and then she cried. Papa said that they would request permission to accompany me to Peking and see me off on the train to Canton. "It is so difficult to get excused from work, and your leaving will give us an opportunity to take a holiday."

Even that night we had little to say to each other and I went upstairs to plan my three remaining days in Tientsin. I packed my best outfit, which I had been saving for my first meeting with Mother: my green skirt, which was three years old but still without patches, and a white blouse made from a pillowcase. And then I cleaned my room until it was time for bed. The next day I put the rest of the house in order, washed the floors and did the laundry. On the second day, I chipped as much coal as I could. This was my job, and I wanted to complete it before I left. The coal was stacked in the yard and each piece was as big as the circle of my arms. I used an ax to break the coal until each piece was smaller than my fist.

On the night before I was to leave for Peking, Skinny Monkey and her family invited me to dinner. I was embarrassed by their generosity, but I could not refuse their invitation. The Lees served a delicious meal, one I shall never forget; they sacrificed one of their two precious chickens for me. It had been many years since I had seen a whole chicken. Now this family would miss half of their egg supply on my account.

After dinner Skinny Monkey and I talked excitedly, and yet not unaware of the sadness of parting. She kept insisting that I was born under some lucky stars, because on the very next day our class was scheduled to go into the countryside for farm work. I giggled but silently agreed. When it was time for me to go, she gave me a present. It was a tin box painted with red flowers. "It will be just the right size for your pass and other important papers." I cried a little. As she walked me home along the route we had traveled so many times, she said, "Sansan, although you have a visitor's pass to Hong Kong, I know your mother will take you home with her. If in another country you have a chance to go to college, I want you to do well, not only for yourself but for all of us who cannot go. Will you promise me that?" Solemnly I vowed I would.

The next morning, I had just time enough to visit Grandmother. I arrived early and found Goo Ma still at home.

"Goo Ma, I have come to bid you farewell. I am leaving for Hong Kong."

Without even turning her head, she said, "I am busy. You had better go."

"But you don't understand—I am going to see my mother."

"OK, OK. 'Bye," and she slammed the door as she marched off to work. She didn't have a single word for her brother or his family.

I ran down the stairs to Grandmother, who was still in bed, and told her that I was leaving that afternoon. She was not at all surprised.

"Ever since your father wrote, I have been confident that you would be reunited with your family. Even if my daughter went to the Safety Bureau to raise questions about you, I knew she would not succeed. Don't mind Goo Ma now. You are going to return home and your life will be full and beautiful. I have no doubt that the future will bring only happiness. Nothing can ever be truly wrong when you are with your own family. But for an old, old woman, will you honor one wish?"

"Of course, Grandmother, anything. Anything."

"Once, many, many years ago, I knew complete happiness. Life was full and my entire family was with me. During this time I wanted to have a picture taken of all of us, and a photographer came to the house and captured our happiness on film. Within ten days three of my children died from scarlet fever. Sansan, the gods envied our happiness and stole it away. Promise me, child, that you will never have a picture taken with your mother, father and two sisters. For then the gods will surely be jealous of your great joy and take it away."

Chapter Ten

As I waited in line to step off the train onto the platform of the Canton station, I clutched my book bags and peered anxiously above shoulders and heads to find the man Mother had sent to meet me. Even though I had no idea how he would look, I was certain I would know him. He would be the only one there who knew me, and our secret would be a sure sign.

I stepped off the train into a confusion of noise and people and baggage. I looked for the man, but no one around me seemed likely. I didn't look for long—he would find me—for I had to get to the Hong Kong ticket window. I asked the conductor, he pointed to the left, and I pushed my way through the crowd in that direction. There were many ticket windows arranged in a large semicircle, but I soon spotted the sign "HONG KONG," and the people waiting on line. As I awaited my turn, I glanced around again for the man. When I reached the window, the ticket seller told me that there were no more express seats left for the next day. I was disappointed, but bought a ticket on the local.

I breathed more easily now that I had a seat on

the train, but still I could not locate the man. The station had cleared, and only a few passengers and some peddlers remained. I walked up and down looking for him, but no one approached me. I was becoming angry. This man was paid well to greet me, he had a picture of me, he knew what I was going to be wearing, he knew about my school badge—and yet somehow he had missed me. Over an hour passed, and I decided to forget about him and make my own arrangements for the night. I went to the hotel-reservations window and asked for a room, but the clerk did not understand me, as he only spoke Cantonese. I tried slowly again: "I want a room for tonight." He said something, and all I could do was nod. He spoke a few more words and then took a yuan from me. I suspected that for a yuan he was selling me a very cheap hotel room; he saw that I was a student and probably didn't think I could afford any more. After I got the hotel ticket, I waited for the post office to open at one-thirty so I could call Mother in Hong Kong.

Finally it opened and I placed my call. I had remained calm and mature despite the frustrations of the missing man, the local train and the Cantonese clerk, but as soon as I uttered "Mother?" over the phone and heard her for the first time call my name, I became her small, small child who could only cry compulsively to express all I wanted her to know. Throughout the call, I sobbed. Her voice pleaded with me to stop. "Everything is all right now. Don't worry,

Sansan, we will be together soon. We only have to wait one more day.'' But while Mother repeated these assurances, she felt as helpless as I did, and was weeping openly.

The sixteen years we had lost was bridged with our first conversation; the unnatural gap was closed simply and forever. Our hearts had reached out and found each other.

After the call I went to the hotel. The manager was rude and would not show me to my room, or even to the staircase. Like a fool, he didn't want to help anyone who was not a Cantonese. So I told him that my parents were Cantonese and therefore I was Cantonese. He was surprised and asked, ''How come you don't speak any Cantonese?'' I told him that my parents moved to the north when I was very small and therefore I had never learned to speak the dialect, and that my grandmother came from very nearby. He believed me and began to feel very sorry for a poor Cantonese girl who had never learned how to speak her own dialect. Now he was very helpful and showed me to my room.

The room was very cheap, just as I had suspected. It was on the second floor, and much smaller than my own room in Tientsin. There was neither glass nor curtains in the window, and the furniture consisted of a small table and a board with a sleeping mat on it.

Canton was very hot and the hotel was stuffy, so I quickly changed my clothes and went outside for a walk. As I strolled around the block, I tried to keep my mind on the store windows and the prices of articles, in order to remain calm and reasonable for the next day's trip. It was no use—my thoughts continually wandered to Mother, who was now less than one hundred miles away. I was angry at myself for crying so hard on the phone and not being able to say anything to her. I couldn't keep my excitement down and hopped a little bit as I walked around the block.

It was time for supper, but I wasn't hungry at all and just bought two bottles of soda to keep cool. I thought about going to a movie to pass away the night, but I didn't know where the theaters were, and I was afraid of getting lost in a town of Cantonese-speaking people. Besides, the man might have called Mother, and she would have sent him to get me.

I thought about calling her again. I still had much money, and a telephone call was only seven yuan. But when I reached the post office, it had already closed for the night. I went back to my hotel.

I had spent little since I left Peking and had over forty yuan left from the amount that Mama and Grandmother had given her. I decided to send most of it back to Tientsin. Even though Mama might be hurt to receive back such a considerable sum, I enclosed it with a lie. I said that the man Mother sent to meet me had given me some money.

When I finished the note, I decided to write a letter to Big Nose, who had hurt me more and made me angrier than anyone else I knew. How could I have known him so well for six years and never suspected that he could do such a thing to me? How could I have been so stupid as not to know his heart? Big Nose had made me realize how narrow my life had been. Before he had raised the six items against me, I thought I had experienced a good deal for my age; after all, I had lived sixteen years without a family and had acquired sharp eyes. I thought I could tell at one glance the motives of a stranger, but in fact I couldn't even see through Big Nose.

I took out his note and reread it.

DEAR CHIN-YEE:

In the time that you have ignored me I cannot tell you how uncomfortable and depressed I have been. When I criticized you, I never thought that you would be angry.

Please forgive me.

I picked up a pen and wrote back:

DEAR COMRADE TSIANG:

Whether you are right or not, you have greatly impressed me. If you are right, then I shall change. If you are not, I shall always remember the six items. You can be sure that five minutes before I die, I shall be thinking about your criticism.

I hope you shall always be running in the front lines of the Socialist March.

After I signed my name, I felt much much better. Big Nose had taught me a great lesson. From then on I would never look into faces with such a simple trust.

I tried to go to sleep, but the night was too hot, and I got up and went down to the lobby for the breeze. There I found an old woman who was living in the hotel. We fell into conversation and compared goods, prices and coupons in Canton and Tientsin, and decided that in Canton there was much more food available than in other areas. After a while, I explained to her that I was leaving the next day and would like to give her some items that I was not taking with me. I went upstairs and brought them down.

She took my books, but was hesitant about the medicine. Laxatives were an everyday necessity for practically everyone on a diet of little oil and harsh corn-husk muffins, but many Cantonese don't like to receive gifts of medicine. They are superstitious and think it is a premonition of sickness. I assured her that I had no need of the medicine and that if she didn't want it, she could merely throw it away. She finally believed me and thanked me for my gifts.

By this time it was late and I was tired. I fell asleep and awoke very early the next morning. Although the train was not leaving until nine-thirty, I was at the station by seven. It was uncrowded, with only a few beggars sleeping on the floor. I found the platform for the local to Hong Kong, and there I met the pockmarked man from the Peking train. As soon as we caught sight of each other's face, we immediately burst into laughter. We had both lied about our destination, for he too was leaving China. We sat together and waited for the train.

In our conversation I told him that I had sent back all my coupons and money and had given away what I didn't need. He was alarmed and said:

"What did you do that for? What if you don't get across to Hong Kong? Don't you realize that many people are turned away every day by the Hong Kong officials?"

"No. I thought that as long as I have my pass from school . . ."

"Don't you know that there are many checkpoints and many people every day don't pass through them? What are you going to do without coupons and money if you don't get into Hong Kong?"

For the first time I was scared. I had never thought about the possibility that the Hong Kong authorities would not let me in. I had believed I planned everything so well, and now I realized how foolish I was to send everything back.

"Don't worry too much. I have one hundred yuan and I will be happy to give you some if you need it."

The ugly young man was very kind, but I knew I couldn't take money from a stranger, and continued to worry about the coming hours.

The train to Hong Kong arrived on time and we boarded it together. The car was full but many people got off at the local stations before we reached the border. A delicious lunch was served on the train. I had rice, eggs and cucumbers. My friend insisted on treating me as I had only five yuan left.

As more and more people got off the train, I began worrying again about the Hong Kong authorities and the possibility that they might keep me out. I would have no money for food or hotel. I wouldn't even have enough for a phone call. I wouldn't be able to go anywhere. I didn't speak Cantonese. I knew that the people in Hong Kong spoke Cantonese and feared that the authorities would not let me in because I spoke only Mandarin. My mind was clouded with a thousand dangers. I was so close to Mother, and yet we might still never meet.

Finally, the train choked to a stop in Shumchün, at the border. As I waited my turn to disembark, I peered out the windows and saw a station crowded with hundreds, perhaps thousands of refugees, the majority pushing toward inspection posts, slowed down only by their bundles and very young or very old family members. But many had sat to rest on their worldly possessions, probably waiting for another attempt to pass the various checkpoints. My pockmarked friend became very tense and worried at the sight of those who had been turned back. He looked to me and pleaded for a favor. ''As a student you will probably have no trouble getting into Hong Kong, but I am afraid my chances are very small. My only hope is for my relatives to come and claim me as part of their family, but we have never met. If you will get this picture to them, they can come and identify me. They live at thirty-three Ho Ho Place. Please, will you do this great favor?" I memorized the address and promised to get the picture to his relatives. He thanked me many times and, shaking hands, we separated as we stepped off the train.

The crowd of barefoot people poured around the inspectors and I followed. There was no line, only pushing bunches of desperate people with anxious faces. As I got closer and closer to the inspector's voice, I became more and more nervous. His harsh tones fired questions at the refugees without relief and if a person hesitated at all in his answer, he was not allowed to pass that checkpoint. I rehearsed my answers over and over again. I was terrified that I would become mute. Over and over—"Soo Chin-yee, student of Teachers' School, Tientsin, thirty-day pass from Safety Bureau to visit sick mother in Hong Kong . . . Soo Chin-yee, student of Teachers' School . . ."

Suddenly I was before the inspector.

"Proof of vaccination."

"Please, Comrade?"

"Proof of vaccination and hurry it up."

"I have been vaccinated but I didn't know I had to have proof."

"No proof, six days' delay, OK, next?"

I grabbed my schoolbag and stood firm.

"Please, I can't. I can't wait six days. No money, no coupons. I have no place to go. Please. I am a student, I had my vaccination at school like all students. Please, I can't wait six days."

"OK, OK, go ahead." He stamped my blue pass and waved me on.

Again I was part of the groping crowd. None of us seemed to be walking with our own feet, but rather propelled by the people around us. Not walking, not running, but somewhere in between, yet it was more tiring than sprinting. Cloth bundles tightly gripped in hand. Eyes darting with fear. My heart was beating so fast I was sure everyone heard it too.

At the second checkpoint I was given three Hong Kong dollars in exchange for my mainland currency.

Then back with the others; only this time we seemed to wait longer than before. When I reached the inspectors, they asked me to show all of my belongings on the table before them. I had carefully put twenty-five safety pins on my schoolbag so that nothing would fall out, and it seemed that I took hours to undo them. The inspectors were annoyed and my fingers shook.

At last, I emptied the contents on the table: my entire wardrobe of a three-year-old brown skirt, two worn white blouses, three pairs of underwear that Mother had sent me from America, a sanitary napkin, a package of high-quality cookies, and Skinny Monkey's tin box.

The inspector handled my clothing carelessly but thoroughly. Then he spotted the ring on my hand that Mama had given me.

"Let's see that ring!" I pulled at the ring, but

in the excitement my finger was wet with perspiration and the ring came off only after a struggle. He looked at it and then gave it back. It was not an expensive ring.

"Do you have any more jewelry?"

"No, that's all. If you want the ring, you may keep it."

A sly smile crept across his face and he turned toward his companions. "Hey, young girl, are you positive you have no more jewelry? There are a lot of hiding places under your clothes."

"I tell you, I have nothing else. Please. I have nothing else."

The man then shifted his weight, sat at the edge of the table and leaned forward toward me.

"I don't believe you. Better take off your blouse so I can see for myself."

Up to then I had been frightened, but as I looked at his smirking face I was overcome by fury and, without thinking, shouted back:

"Comrade, I am not hiding anything!"

"What if we find something?"

I shouted back, "What if you don't! What then? How are you going to explain your actions to your superiors? How will they know you simply did not want me to undress? I am a teacher, an important member of socialism."

Surprised by my sharp tongue, he let me go on. When I realized that I had actually intimidated the inspector, I almost fainted. But now I was practically across the bridge, with only one checkpoint separating me from Hong Kong and my mother. I was behind a large family of brothers and sisters at the next checkpoint. I couldn't hear what was being said. All six members were allowed through, except for the smallest child, who was left behind. I saw her crying as the inspector briskly asked me in Cantonese for my identification.

He looked over my pass and noticed my school badge. Then he said, "Hung la, hung la!" I didn't understand and stood staring at his mouth. He repeated, "Hung la, hung la!" I was frozen. Then the man behind me said, "Run, run, you can go. Run."

I grabbed my paper and my bag and ran toward the bridge. The bridge was crowded and again I was lost within the people's anxious surge across the fifty yards. I couldn't see over their heads, I could only hear the young child crying for his family behind me.

Ahead of me was the first Hong Kong checkpoint. This time the inspectors were English, with a Chinese translator beside them.

I rehearsed my answers again and again. I remembered what Mother had said about giving Papa's name and a false address in Hong Kong. For the first time I had to lie and I was afraid.

The Englishman was tall—all I could see was a pair of dark sunglasses and a huge hooked nose. He uttered something. The Chinese translator then asked me:

"Whom do you want to see in Hong Kong?"

"My mother and my family."

He repeated my answer to the proud Englishman and then asked me:

"What relatives live in Hong Kong?"

"Mother, father and two sisters."

"Whom are you leaving behind in China?"

"No one. I was the only one in China."

"Why are you going to Hong Kong?"

"My mother is sick and I am on summer vacation from school."

"Who is your father?"

"Soo Yu-ting."

He then waved me on to the next inspector, who asked me the same questions. I thought they must be double-checking my answers. I really believed they were going to turn me back when the inspector asked me for my father's address. I repeated the address Mother had given me and was sure they were going to check it. Instead, I was passed on.

I purchased a ticket and got on the shuttle train to the city. After I found a seat and the train started to move, I realized that I hadn't eaten very much in the past few days and suddenly became starved. To make matters worse, a peddler marched up and down the aisle calling, "Cakes, milk, candy. Cakes, milk, candy."

Finally, after about an hour, the train stopped and I rushed out of the car, the last one, and I ran through the crowd on the platform toward the center of the station, trying to avoid bumping into the other people, several times colliding with strangers, both of us anxious to find someone and not paying attention, muttering "Excuse me," and as I got closer to the station building, I heard a voice call, "Sansan, Sansan . . ."

and I knew it could only be my mother, and suddenly we saw each other and were in each other's arms.

Afterword

The only memory I had of my sister Sansan before the night of October 18, 1962, was of a baby dressed in pink wool, waving good-bye to us from the Shanghai pier. Yet our reunion at New York International Airport some sixteen years later was not at all strained or strange. Our words and tears flowed freely. The only odd sensation I experienced was seeing someone who looked very much like me. I soon discovered we were alike in many other ways.

That entire night was spent trying to out-talk one another, as we quickly and naturally closed the gap. I began to share her life from her earliest memories to those few first hours in Hong Kong.

Although Mother had spoken to Sansan on the telephone, when she arrived at the station in Hong Kong she still feared that something might have gone wrong at the last moment. She waited many hours in the August heat, staving off panic as several border trains arrived without Sansan. Finally, at about four in the afternoon, the merchant my mother had paid handsomely to guide Sansan from Canton to Hong Kong appeared with a long face and said, "I am terribly sorry. I could not find your daughter. She has not been able to get out." My mother glanced over his shoulder and cried, "Then tell me who is that behind you? Sansan . . . Sansan . . ."

Mother and daughter wept in each other's arms for over an hour. Suddenly Sansan realized that she had not yet really seen her mother, and she stepped back to take a good look. Instead of a sickly woman close to her fifties, Sansan saw instead her youthful and lovely mother of the photographs. She soon learned that Mother had only feigned illness as part of her plan to get her to Hong Kong.

This plan was shaped solely by our mother with remarkable intuition and perseverance. During the early part of 1962, when masses of refugees exploded into Hong Kong and the news headlines, Mother sensed that then, if ever, was the time to bring Sansan out. She resolutely mapped out her strategy despite the misgivings of our father and concerned friends, who knew that nothing short of a miracle would bring Sansan safely to Hong Kong, and who feared that the inevitable failure of any plan would break her heart. She knew her chances for success ultimately rested on the whims of the Chinese Communist regime, which sometimes inexplicably allowed people to leave. Thus she wrote the three letters which were forwarded to Sansan by friends in Tokyo.

Mother did all that she could from the outside, being careful to include any factor that might influence the authorities, including our status of an overseas Chinese family in international business, appealing to the Communists' hunger for foreign exchange and international good will. Then she flew to Hong Kong in late June to stand her vigil. In the final analysis we shall never know why the Communists let Sansan go.

Mother swept Sansan back from the railroad station to the hotel where she stripped my sister of her clothing and scrubbed her down from braids to toe. I think she wanted to have a completely fresh, clean start with her youngest daughter. Mother then wanted to burn Sansan's pillowcase blouse and other worn clothing, but Sansan cried, ''No, we must send them back; they will be needed.'' The few pieces of clothing were wrapped and mailed back to Tientsin.

On August 18, 1962, two miracles happened to our family. Not only was Sansan able to rejoin us after a separation of sixteen years, but she immediately and naturally took her place as one of the family.

Mother and Sansan stayed a week in Hong Kong to await the next refugee boat to Taiwan, where Sansan was greeted by our father. They remained in Taiwan until October, awaiting visa clearance to the United States, and then flew by way of Japan to New York.

Once home, Sansan was as eager as I to start on a book about her life in China. Ever since she left the Mainland, she realized that her life was wholly different from the lives of other girls in this and other countries, and she wanted to tell her story. We began taping sessions immediately, at first monologues by Sansan, then interviews with me. The general outline began forming in my mind as I translated the tapes from Chinese and transcribed them. I organized the more than 250 pages of notes and began to write. I kept going back to Sansan with questions and interviews, and we worked closely until the book was completed.

Sansan's book ends with her reunion with Mother, but her story continues. Though there never were any of the major adjustment problems one would imagine for her in the United States, our family has witnessed some subtle and important changes in her. Sansan has mellowed and is less sensitive to others' words and actions. She is less suspicious of others and has learned to laugh at herself.

The credit for her relatively easy adjustment must fall to our parents and to Sansan herself. Mother has tutored her in getting along with others, and Father has labored for a minimum of two hours a day on her English and school work. And fundamental to the transition, of course, is the fact that Sansan left China only to be with her parents, and thus her life is full.

Her worries now are small and often quite comical. She is attending public high school and works very hard to achieve good grades. She has made many friends in the town, and they have made her feel at home. But English occasionally still puzzles her. In her eagerness to apply newly-learned idioms, "Keep cool" became "Keep chilly," and "I am in a pickle" came out "I am in a cucumber."

Today her main concern is college. She has never forgotten her promise to Skinny Monkey and is ever mindful of those less fortunate friends she has left behind. While she is sometimes awed by the future, she is secure in the knowledge that at last it is her own.

BETTE BAO LORD was born in Shanghai in 1938, and her sister, SANSAN, seven years later in Chungking. In 1946, their father was assigned to the United States and was shortly joined by his wife and two elder daughters. Sansan, who was only one, remained in China with relatives. Subsequent political events separated Sansan for sixteen years from her true family and even from the knowledge of their existence. *Eighth Moon* is the story of those year's in Sansan's life.

Mrs. Lord lives in New York with her husband, Winston Lord, who is now president of the Council on Foreign Relations, and their two children, Lisa and Winston. She is also the author of the bestselling novel, *Spring Moon*.

Sansan graduated from Tufts University with a degree in mathematics. She now lives in Washington, D.C., and works as a pension expert for a private firm.